SLANDER & PSYCHICS

MRS. POMOLO INVESTIGATES

DONNA MUSE

CLICK HERE to Join our Reader's Club and to Receive Tica House Updates!

https://cozymystery.subscribemenow.com/

CONTENTS

[1]

Serenity Sparklan had sprung up right at seven, just seconds before her alarm clock went off. She had taken a ten-minute shower and thrown on a comfortable, if unflattering, pair of sweatpants and an Ohio State hoodie over a worn tee. She made herself a smoothie of raspberries, pineapple, kiwi, and papaya in the blender and then, because it was still too chilly to be jogging outside—and also, though she would never admit this, because she feared for her own safety—she ran laps around the house.

This done, she flung herself down onto the sofa and booted up the laptop.

For the past six months, ever since the incident in Columbus, Serenity had been working as a gossip columnist for the Wrangler's Hill *Beacon*. The *Beacon* hadn't had a gossip columnist before Serenity showed up in the executive editor's office one morning wearing a forbidding pastel pantsuit and a smile that would have unnerved a gorilla. Her journalism teacher in high school had once told her that what Serenity lacked in social awareness, she made up for in her ability to bully people into getting whatever she wanted. He hadn't meant it as a compliment, but Serenity had taken it as one. By the time Serenity emerged from the office at the end of that meeting, the *Beacon* had added a new weekly column and a new writer.

Serenity logged onto Twitter, where she would spend much of the morning doing keyword searches to see what people were discussing in Wrangler's Hill. Shortly after moving to town, she had subscribed to all the local Facebook groups so she could follow drama as it unfolded. She had already been booted from several—but no matter. A creature of the internet from the time she had been old enough to click "subscribe," Serenity had a supernatural gift for acquiring information even when others were doing their best to keep her from getting it.

If there was one thing Serenity was good at, it was antagonizing people. Just before retiring to bed the night before, she had followed a dozen new accounts, including the head of the Department of Waste Management and the manager of the Cold Stones on East and Burridge. When she checked her follows this morning, she found out the manager of the Cold Stones and four of the other accounts had blocked her.

Despite having lived here for less than a year, Serenity had already acquired something of a reputation. Her options for coffee were growing increasingly limited because the cashiers at three of the local coffee houses refused to serve her. And nowhere was she more hated than at work, which is why she had recently given up going to the office in favor of working from home. Veronica, her editor, had agreed to the change readily; none of the other reporters seemed to like working with her, least of all Evelyn Rider, the fashion and lifestyle columnist with the ridiculous geyser of flaming, carrot-colored hair bursting from the top of her head. She had complained to HR when Serenity had started a Google doc listing everyone on staff who was "problematic."

"She's trying to get people fired for trivial offenses," Evelyn had complained to Veronica, her red hair bobbing like a fishing lure. "Doris caught her scrolling through tweets that Doris had 'faved' six years ago to see if she had any views that could get her in trouble with the company."

"To be fair," said Serenity smoothly, "I made it so anyone could edit that document. I wanted people to list co-workers who might have problematic views. I thought it could be a collaborative effort."

Somehow, this explanation had not gone over well with her fellow employees.

"This woman," said Evelyn, her face turning the color of her hair, "is a parody of everything that's wrong with the younger generation of reporters. If it were left up to her, we'd all be fired for things we did or said twenty years ago. She's trying to lead a purge of her competitors, and she's doing it under the cover of being a Miss Goody-Goody."

Veronica listened patiently until she had finished, then turned to Serenity and said, "Serenity, delete the document. Please."

"But—"

"I don't want to hear any buts. I'm sure you had good intentions, but this spreadsheet has caused too many problems already. If this newspaper is going to function properly, we can't have all this backstabbing and infighting. Frankly, I'm too busy to care what people were faving on Twitter in 2012. I think you all spend too much time on that cursed website as it is."

"Twitter is an essential tool of the modern journalist," said Serenity, not for the first, nor the last time. "It's hard to do our jobs without it."

"I don't see you doing your jobs," said Veronica wearily. "I see you all sharing memes seven, eight hours a day." She waved a dismissive hand, as if to signal the conversation was over. "Enough. If you manage to find video footage of someone in this office pledging allegiance to ISIS, then by all means show me. Otherwise, I give neither hoot nor holler what you do in your free time."

She escorted both Serenity and Evelyn to the door before they could put in another word.

"Well, I suppose you got what you wanted," said Serenity coldly as they made their way back to their desks.

"I suppose I did," said Evelyn mildly; she looked as though she could desperately use another cup of coffee. "Back to writing obituaries."

What followed was still a matter of some debate in the office. Serenity swore—and had written a memo to HR insisting—that she had shrugged nonchalantly and said, "I guess death comes for us all in the end."

But Evelyn—and here she was backed by two other people —had heard something altogether different. According to them, Serenity had whipped sharply round and said in a low, indignant voice, "Then I guess you had better stop getting in the way of me doing my job, or they'll be writing *yours* next."

———

For twelve years, Iris Reeves had been a member in good standing of the Wrangler's Hill Horticulture and Gardening Club. But then last December, Flora Hortescue had been elected the club's president, and had quietly but rapidly begun turning everyone against Iris.

Iris first noticed something was amiss one Thursday evening in mid-January when she arrived at a diner's buffet room which was being temporarily used as the clubhouse ten minutes late, having accidentally caused a small grease fire while trying to make salmon in her home kitchen. The rest of the club, some two dozen women ranging in age from forty to seventy-two, were already seated eating or making their way through a buffet line consisting of homemade macaroni, potato salad, ribs, brisket, coleslaw, chicken fried stick and mashed potatoes. The smell struck Iris with potent force as she entered the room, reminding her of summer grass and the tang of her aunt Bethel's too-sour lemonade.

But it wasn't the food that commanded her attention.

Almost from the moment she entered, to a person the room fell silent. Iris had the uncanny suspicion that they had been talking about her just a second before. The faces that in previous years had perked up in welcome when she entered, now looked disapproving and downcast. As she made her way to the buffet table at the back of the room, she was conscious of the fact that everyone was either looking at her or studiously attempting not to.

"Evening, Gladys," Iris said cheerily. "Evening, Helga." But neither Gladys nor Helga replied.

It didn't take Iris long to figure out who was responsible. Flora had never much liked Iris, but the moment she ascended to the presidency of the club following the sudden death of Vera Rosenthorpe, she had made it her personal mission to expel Iris from the club.

Under questioning, Helga finally broke down and admitted that Flora had been meeting with each of her fellow members in private and spreading salacious gossip. "She says you were once seen at a sleazy night club in high heels," said Helga, "and that you wear wearing gaudy make-up an inch thick, and that you've been known to date numerous men almost simultaneously."

"Well, even if that was true, what of it?" said Iris. "I don't see that it's any of her business, or anyone else's."

But this proved to be the wrong thing to say. Never mind that half the women in the club had done the same or worse at some point—now that Flora was in charge, the women had suddenly and belatedly rediscovered their commitment to Uptight Morals and Extreme Decency. And that meant, first of all, censuring Iris for her offenses against both.

For not a week later, an emergency meeting was called.

"Iris Reeves," said Flora when the group convened, "you have been seen acting inappropriately and indecently... not to our understood standards. You know we're not riffraff in this club, nor do we tolerate it. We have our reputation to think of. We are a conservative group, and we simply do not dally in such evil things like a yoga class in skimpy noth-ings... nor do we frequent places that condone heavy music with ghastly lyrics. Do you have anything to say for yourself?"

Iris blinked and bit her tongue to keep from pointing out the absurdity of the situation. She was seated on a hard-backed wooden chair amongst the others in the circle, feeling oddly like Joan of Arc in front of an Inquisition of old biddies. The other twenty-four women sat around her with their expressionless faces veiled in shadow. In the pocket of her blouse, Iris had tucked the Red Carnation, a polyester flower which she had been presented on her initiation into the club twelve years before and had been worn to every meeting since.

"Some of your information is questionable," said Iris. "I haven't just gone to yoga *once* as you're implying, I go every week. I have a club membership."

This news was punctuated by murmurs and clucking, as if all the women in the club were gnashing their teeth together at the same time.

"Hmmph!" said Flora. "There you have it, girls. Iris has a proud spirit, a sassy tongue, and an apparent refusal to listen to or abide by our standards."

Dolores, the secretary, hurried to scribble down the new accusations in her steno notepad.

"Iris," said Flora, "you have gone against us, against humanity, and against good taste. I move that you be ousted, forbidding you from rejoining our club in perpetuity."

"Seconded," came a voice from somewhere to the right of Iris—when she recalled the meeting later, Iris couldn't remember whether it was Priscilla Morales or Petunia Mossley.

"All who are in favor," said Flora, raising her hand.

Without hesitation everyone in the room raised their hands —Helga, last of all, and somewhat reluctantly. "Sorry," she mouthed to Iris with a penitent look. Iris shot a withering look at Flora, wondering what the snooty woman had done to threaten her one remaining friend.

Flora made a great show of counting all the raised hands; then, with a look of deep joy and satisfaction, she strode forward and snatched the Red Carnation out of Iris's shirt pocket, tossing it behind her. "Iris, by unanimous consent, you're ousted from this club forever. If you so much as attempt to set foot into our meetings again, we'll... we'll..."

Or course, there was nothing she could threaten Iris with, for the club wasn't even a legal entity, simply a group of women who'd been together forever in the name of gardening.

"The prohibition extends to the end of your natural life," Flora concluded.

"And beyond, if we can manage it," said Gladys, and everyone laughed. Iris had a sudden, horrible vision of the Wrangler's Hill Horticulture and Gardening Club collectively lobbying St. Peter to deny her entrance into heaven.

[2]

WHEN IRIS RETURNED HOME that evening, her house-mate, Geneva Pomolo, poured her a cup of coffee and listened in restrained silence as she recounted the events of the meetings.

"I hate them," said Iris. "I hate them all, and what's more, I would like them to let me back into the club."

Sitting on the sofa with her legs tucked under her pleated skirt, she had the look of a pigeon brooding over a nest of eggs. Geneva clucked her tongue in disapproval. "Honestly, Iris," she said, "you're too good for them. I've never heard of anything so ludicrous. They're a bunch of snobbish, bored women—excluding you, of course. Perhaps your energy would be better spent finding a new club where you're welcomed and valued."

"No, I want them to suffer for giving me the boot," said Iris, rattling her jangly bracelet. "They deserve to be punished by having to be continually reminded of my existence. I want them to wail in despair when they see me coming. I want them to shake their fists at the sky."

Geneva could see that it was going to take Iris some time to get over this latest social humiliation. This wasn't the first time she had been forcibly ejected from a group for seemingly inscrutable reasons: Iris was a brassy, opinionated, sharp-tongued woman, and had something of a gift for drawing the scorn of more conventional people who resented her colorful personality. She had once been ejected from a group dinner for admitting that she had enjoyed Beyoncé's performance during the Super Bowl half-time show.

"They want to silence me," said Iris, "but I won't be silenced. I'm thinking about applying for a job at the Beacon so that they have to read my reporting or opinions day in and day out."

"That's actually a great idea," said Geneva, who had long been lobbying Iris to leave her low-paying job at the city water department. "If you managed to get one of your mystery novels published, that would really show 'em."

Iris had spent much of the past year writing a mystery novel in her spare moments; recently, she had purchased a vintage typewriter and sometimes late at night, Geneva could hear her clacking away in the other room while she was trying to sleep. (Iris's energy was indefatigable, and this seemed to annoy her critics as much as anything.)

"The nice thing about living in a town this small," said Iris, tapping her nails on the mug's rim, "is that they can't get rid of me entirely, not unless they murder me. And if they did, I have every confidence that you would apprehend them accordingly."

Since retiring from teaching, Geneva had been working full-time as a private investigator, often helping the Wrangler's Hill's Police Department. During her off hours, Iris worked as Geneva's assistant and right-hand woman, which mostly amounted to driving her around and protecting her from suspects if they grew too unruly. (Geneva had once nearly been killed by a flying harpoon.)

"I bet I know something that might cheer you up," said Geneva, eager to leave the subject of Iris's murder. "There's a writer's symposium being held next week at the Hilton. Roman Koistinen will be the featured speaker—"

Iris sprang half out of her seat. "You mean he's coming to town and no one told me?"

"You know him?" asked Geneva, looking pleased to have diverted Iris's attention from thoughts of revenge.

"Know him? He's written practically every major book on the craft of writing—*Write a Bestseller in One Week, Plotting Made Perfect, Novel-Writing Ninja, Mapping Your Masterpiece*..."

"Okay, but what has he written?"

Iris sank back onto the sofa, gazing at her blankly. "Written? I just told you."

"Surely, he's written, like, an actual novel or a movie or something?"

Iris was silent.

"Well, anyway," said Geneva, "the conference is next weekend and tickets are thirty-five dollars. I don't have anything going on that weekend, Lord willing. I'd be happy to pay your ticket. Consider it a consolation present for being thrown out of the gardening club."

"Gen, dear, you don't have to do that," said Iris, looking faintly pleased. "I could actually pitch this to the *Beacon* and maybe they'd pay me to cover it. Tell you what: if I manage to land this assignment, I'll pay you back with the money they give me."

"Don't even worry about it," said Geneva, rising from her chair and heading back into the kitchen for a second cup of coffee. "I'm mostly curious to see whether this 'celebrated author' has anything useful to say on the craft of writing."

"He's full of practical advice," said Iris, a little defensively. "He taught me all about the importance of making sure at least one character has a gun. I wouldn't have gotten anywhere in my book if it weren't for him."

"And just how far have you gotten in your book?" said Geneva slyly.

Again, Iris was silent.

[3]

The Incredible Claudia, professional psychic, was preparing for a mid-afternoon appointment. She had recently taken to mixing an entire can of Sleep-No-More energy drinks with a shot of lemonade before meeting with clients, which had the effect of dilating her eyes slightly and making her seem even more mystical and eerie. She was just draining the last of her glass when her assistant, twenty-year-old Mary Anne Steenblik, timidly entered.

"Sorry to interrupt," she said. "Mrs. Adams is waiting for you in the lobby."

"Tell her I'll be out in a few moments." Placing a turban on her head with a ruby in its center, Claudia turned round. "What do you think? Does it give the desired effect?"

Mary Anne had learned that Claudia hated when she wasn't forthright. "I-If you don't mind my saying so," she stammered, "I prefer the peacock feather. The one that makes you look like Cyd Charisse."

"Peacock feather it is, then," said Claudia, tucking the feather behind her ear and combing her hair back. "Better?"

Mary Anne smiled. "You look like the world's most gifted psychic."

With a feeling of satisfaction, Claudia seated herself at the circular table and motioned for Mrs. Adams to be brought into the room. She entered after some coaxing, clutching her purse to her chest a little nervously and looking over-awed, which suggested to Claudia that she had never before consulted the services of a professional psychic.

"I'll admit, you're not like any psychic I've seen on TV," said Mrs. Adams. "Where are your tarot cards and crystal ball? Where are the clouds of smoky incense?"

"I can light a candle if it would help you to focus," said Claudia genially. "Crystal balls are just tools—some would say props. I don't use them because I don't need them."

This information seemed to reassure Mrs. Adams, as it was intended to do.

"If you wouldn't mind closing your eyes, though," said Claudia, "we'll spend the next few minutes meditating in silence."

Reluctantly the woman shut her eyes, though she continued to clutch tightly to her purse as if worried that Claudia was going to snatch it discreetly out of her hand and look through it. When Claudia judged that she was sufficiently relaxed, she said quietly, "You're very lonely. Particularly lately."

Mrs. Adams nodded, looking faintly impressed.

Encouraged, Claudia added, "You've recently lost someone, someone of tremendous importance. You and he had grown so close that losing him was like losing a part of yourself."

Claudia winced, wishing that she had used the gender-neutral pronoun. Luckily, it didn't seem to matter, for Mrs. Adams sat up in her seat with an impassioned look. "Yes, Richard... he was my husband. Can you see him? Is he in the room with us?"

Claudia shook her head, although Mrs. Adams' eyes remained closed. "No, but you give off an energy of grief and confusion. You understand, don't you, that the visible world is just the surface of the real? There is so much more than what we can see with our eyes."

"Yes, I... I think I see that, now," said Mrs. Adams.

Claudia studied her client carefully. She had the look of someone who dismissed anything smacking of mysticism as superstitious hogwash, so how had she ended up here? Perhaps a friend had nudged her in this direction, or perhaps grief had driven her to desperate extremes.

"But you would tell me, wouldn't you?" Mrs. Adams went on. "You would tell me if Richard came into the room?"

"I would tell you," said Claudia.

"Does that ever happen, that you see spirits?"

Claudia considered the question carefully. There were certain concepts that it was difficult to explain to a layman. "I wouldn't call myself a medium, no," she said. "Every object in the physical realm gives off an energy, Mrs. Adams. You can discern truth from a stone if you know how to read it properly. We must guard our dreams carefully, for if you tell someone your dreams, you're telling them every-thing there is to know about you."

"And I suppose you're simply better at reading things than most people," Mrs. Adams replied.

The heat in the room was becoming oppressive; Claudia was beginning to regret that she had turned up the thermostat.

"I had a dream recently," said Mrs. Adams shyly. "I wasn't going to share this with anyone, but since you brought it up... I was in a farmhouse with a hedgehog—"

But she never disclosed the contents of the dream, for at that moment Claudia let out a terrifying scream that sent Mrs. Adams leaping out of her seat.

"Claudia?" said Mrs. Adams, making a bold attempt to keep her fear in check. "Claudia, are you all right?"

But Claudia didn't answer. She was trembling visibly; her peacock feather flapped in agitation as though seeking a means of escape; her face had turned an unpleasant plum color, as of someone being strangled. She no longer seemed to be looking at Mrs. Adams, but past her to the door. Mrs. Adams turned around, half expecting to see the corporeal form of her husband standing there, but there was no one there.

"My dear woman," said Mrs. Adams, beginning to get really angry, "if this is a performance, I must insist—"

But Claudia spoke over her.

"This has never happened before," she said in a tone both low and urgent, "but a man has entered the room. He's moving toward you. He is standing even now at your left elbow."

Despite her general feeling of skepticism, Mrs. Adams was so overcome by the force of Claudia's words that she couldn't help but flinch a little and move the chair two or three inches to the right.

"Do I know him?" she asked. "What does he look like?"

Claudia gazed in rapt silence for a moment. "He's wearing a dark homburg and a tweed vest. His Oxford brogues are a little scuffed around the edges, as though in need of a polish. He's looking over at you with a look of deep if ineffectual tenderness."

Some of the color began to drain from Mrs. Adams' cheeks. "That's Richard," she said quietly. Her back stiffened; she shut her eyes, as if worrying that he might materialize in front of her. "What does he want?"

Claudia didn't reply right away. Instead, she continued to gaze at a spot just over the woman's shoulders, nodding attentively and occasionally puncturing the silence with an "mmm" or an "mm-hmm." Mrs. Adams looked slightly indignant, with the air of a woman listening to two people speak in a foreign language that she can't understand and knowing they're talking about her.

"Forgive me," said Claudia finally, "I've been at this job for nearly twenty years, but never in all that time has a spirit appeared before me in corporeal form. The most I've ever seen is a vague shape—"

"Did he speak to you?" said Mrs. Adams.

Claudia leaned forward and said in a conspiratorial whisper, "He wanted me to deliver a message."

The use of the past tense suggested to Mrs. Adams that the phantom had gone. "Is he in heaven? Is he happy?"

"It's got nothing to do with that." Reaching her veined hands across the table, Claudia gripped Mrs. Adams by the forearm. "He needs you to understand that you're in terrible danger. The house where you're currently living—the house that the two of you built together—some dark energy has come over it. That energy is attracting some unsavory people. Mrs. Adams, have there been robberies in your neighborhood lately?"

Mrs. Adams looked unnerved by the question. "There was one, not three nights ago. House down the street. First time anything of the sort has ever—"

Claudia cut her off. "They will come for you next. My dear woman, I don't care what it takes, I would advise you to be fully moved out of that house by the end of the week. There are some seriously bad men about, and they want to hurt you. That was what Richard said to me. He said, 'Don't let them hurt her. Her time is not up yet.'"

[4]

By the following Saturday when Geneva and Iris set out for the Hilton, the story of Claudia's extraordinary outburst had been disseminated throughout Wrangler's Hill by an item in the *Beacon's* gossip column. The story had been written in a sensational and hyperbolic manner (at one point Claudia "seemed to rise three feet off the ground, carrying her chair with her"), and public opinion was divided as to whether an event of genuine supernatural import had taken place in her office or whether she was upping the theatrics in the hopes of attracting publicity.

"I'd like to go and speak to the client," said Geneva as they made their way downtown on an unseasonably warm and muggy afternoon. "Perhaps she can tell us what really happened, although by now she may have repeated the story so often that even she would have trouble remembering."

Iris was more inclined to believe stories of ghosts and para-normal occurrences than Geneva, but even she evinced a pronounced skepticism towards professional psychics.

"I'm not saying it can't happen," she said, as she pulled onto the feeder road. "I had a cousin who was a seventh child of a seventh child, and she used to have the most vivid premonitions. Once saved her dad's life, when she warned him not to climb into a tractor. They searched the tractor and found an enormous rattle snake had curled up beneath the brakes."

"Iris, you can't seriously believe this woman," said Geneva, fanning herself with a brochure.

Iris shook her head. "Like I said, I think some people come by the gift naturally. But when it's your job... well, there's a certain financial incentive to play up the drama, isn't there?"

Iris spent several minutes attempting to find a parking space, finally locating one at the far end of the lot in front of a large potted plant where a van had just pulled out. She and Geneva emerged from the car, both wishing they had worn thinner clothing. The scent of smog and oil drifted up over the hill from the city's industrial center.

"I do hope Roman will hang around for a bit after the lecture," said Iris. "I'd love to know whether he thinks it's even possible to write an original mystery plot."

"I keep telling you, originality is overrated," said Geneva as they followed a slow-moving couple through a pair of doors into a spacious lobby. "There are only, I want to say, three possible motives for wanting to murder someone... There are a limited number of murder methods and an equally limited number of ways of concealing a murder. After a century of mystery-writing, I think it's fair to assume that

every possible combination of motive, method and conceal-
ment has been written."

"And that's what worries me," said Iris, reaching to take a
salmon-paste sandwich on a toothpick from a uniformed
man carrying a tray. "Suppose I inadvertently write a story
that someone else has already written?"

"I guarantee you that no one will notice," said Geneva.

"You'd be surprised; mystery-lovers are an obsessive lot..."

By the time they had checked in at the front desk, it was a
quarter to five. The conference room on the second floor
was rapidly filling. "Surely all these people haven't shown
up just to hear this man lecture," said Geneva.

"I don't think you realize how famous he is," replied Iris.

"But what has he *done?* What has he actually written
besides books about how to write books?"

Just ahead of them on the stairs, a woman in a blue blouse
was speaking in low, indignant tones to a bald man in an
immaculately pressed white suit. "I've already told you,"
she said, "if he wanted me to speak, he should have offered
me something by way of compensation."

"Well, you've got about ten minutes to decide," said the man
in the white suit. "But you should know that Mr. Koistinen
is expecting you to introduce him. You can discuss payment
after the conference."

"I'm afraid he's going to be very disappointed, then," said
the woman, removing her glasses briskly and wiping them
down with the hem of her shirt. "I've worked with Roman

long enough to know his tricks. If he doesn't pay you in advance, you don't get paid at all."

Geneva and Iris exchanged significant glances; but they were unable to say anything further, as they had just entered the large conference room.

The two women seated themselves at a circular table near the sound booth that had been draped in white linen, in the center of which stood a vase bearing a single bright chrysanthemum. Geneva glanced round in search of the woman who had been walking in front of them, but she was nowhere to be found. "Did you see her slip out?" she asked Iris.

Iris was busily unwrapping a complimentary chocolate wedge that had been placed on her plate alongside several small cubes of cheese. "Maybe she nipped out to use the loo," she said in a careless tone.

It was now three minutes until the lecture was scheduled to begin. Geneva watched the stage eagerly, waiting to see whether the woman might be cajoled into changing her mind. Right at five, patriotic-sounding music began playing from the loudspeakers near the front of the room and a number of people turned eagerly to watch. However, when another three, then four, then six minutes passed and no one appeared, the level of conversation, which had ebbed at first, returned to a dull murmur. An old man in a tweed cap who was seated in the sound booth said into the microphone, "We're very sorry for the delay, there have been some unexpected technical difficulties backstage."

"Can't imagine what that's about," said Iris dryly.

When the clock on the back wall reached 5:10, a man with thinning hair in a shapeless, ill-fitting grey blazer and checkered pants emerged onto the stage looking distinctly ruffled. In a voice that was just slightly too hearty, he yelled, "Hello everyone. Can't tell you what a privilege it is to see so many of your bright, eager faces peeping back at me."

"I've never seen someone less excited to be getting paid to speak in front of a group of people," murmured Iris.

"No, but he certainly wants us to think he's excited, doesn't he?" said Geneva as he began motioning for everyone in the room to stand and stretch (which she absolutely refused to do).

Once everyone was settled, Mr. Koistinen began divulging his writing approach.

"I want to clear up a common misconception," he said, with the air of a youth pastor dispensing tough wisdom to a roomful of rowdy teens. "People will tell you that other writers are your friends. Other writers are *not* your friends. They are your foes. They are your competitors."

There was a smattering of laughter.

"You people think I'm kidding, but I'm totally serious. You are a leopard, and they are the other leopards attempting to snag the gazelle before you—the gazelle being agents and contracts and book deals and audience. I don't want you to think of other writers as people. I want you to think of them as PREDATORS who are only there to make your life DIFFICULT."

"Is this person for real?" Geneva leaned over and whispered. "Iris, is this the sort of nonsense he puts into those books you read?"

Iris kept her eyes fixed studiously on the lectern and said nothing.

"When I was coming up, back in the stone age," Mr. Koistinen went on, "there was a lot of talk about 'reading widely' and 'reading the classics' to become a better writer. Stephen King famously said he could sum up everything he knew about writing in three words: 'Read, read, read.' I'm here to tell you that's a lot of garbage." He waited for the ensuing commotion to die down before adding, "You are not going to get anywhere as a writer of commercial fiction by reading the Odyssey. You would be better off watching television and going to the movies to get a sense of what people are really interested in today.

"How many of you know who A. W. Cornish is? Everybody?" Geneva and Iris raised their hands, as did most of the people in the room. "In my opinion she's one of the best crime novelists writing today. She tells a story in one of her books on writing. She had a friend who wrote these wonderfully literary novels that were always winning prestigious awards at book festivals and showing up on critics' end-of-the-year lists. This author called up Mrs. Cornish and said, 'I'm just not interested in writing for the masses. I want to write great literature.' and Mrs. Cornish told her, 'Well, that is why you win awards, and I am rich.'"

This time everyone laughed except Iris, who had been mouthing the words as he said them.

"My point in telling you that is this," said Mr. Koistinen. "I'm not here to make you a better writer. I'm here to help you write a bestseller. You might think those two things are connected, and if that's the case, I have a bridge over Lake Alpaca I'd like to sell you." He waited again for the laughter to subside. "The cold truth is this: the more literary your book is, the fewer people are going to want to read it. You have to decide now what you want. Do you want to write a masterpiece that maybe five people read, or do you want to write a gripping story that takes the world by storm?"

AFTER THE LECTURE ENDED, Geneva and Iris went down-stairs into the lobby where Geneva's boyfriend, George Wilson, stood waiting for them. He had brought a bag full of tacos wrapped in shiny foil and glass bottles of apple cider, which they drank over dinner at a table in the crowded dining hall.

"Sorry I couldn't make it to the lecture," he said. "Carol Vargas phoned me upset because the lights in her house kept flickering on and off. Not just one light but all the lights. She thought maybe the neighbor boys were playing a prank, but I drove over there and found a raccoon messing with the breaker box."

"Always the raccoons," said Geneva bitterly.

"You didn't miss much," said Iris, eyeing her nearly empty glass with a gloomy expression. "There was nothing he hadn't already said in *Writing the Breakout Bestseller*. Except at the very end of the lecture he tried to sell us on another, even more expensive lecture series he's giving this summer where he shares writing secrets you 'won't find in books.'"

"Ain't that just the way," said George sadly. "If he gave a lecture on 'how to scam people out of their money,' at least it would be more honest."

"I suppose I'm better off listening to actual novelists." Iris held up the book she had been holding in her lap, a green hardbound copy of *Write Your Way Out of Debt*. "But given that we drove all this way and spent all that money, the least he could do is sign this for me."

"His signature isn't worth the paper it's printed on, honestly," said Geneva, who was still brooding over the insult to the *Odyssey* and hadn't touched a bite of her food. "You'd be better off throwing that book in the bin when you get home. Or we could use the pages to wallpaper the upstairs bathroom."

Iris wasn't listening, however; she had taken out her phone and was scrolling through social media. "Madeline Ponderphelt's family has started a funding campaign to cover her funeral expenses. Neither Benjoram nor Karen is employed at the moment and buying the coffin just about bankrupted them."

"I didn't realize Madeline had died," George said in surprise. He folded up what remained of his taco inside its foil wrap and dropped it inside his tote bag. "She was only in, what, her late fifties?"

"This was about a month ago," said Geneva. "I read you the text—we were watching *The Beast from 20,000 Fathoms*—"

"I must not have heard you." George passed his bottle across the table to Iris, who snatched it up with embarrassing swiftness. "What was the cause?"

"Overdose of anxiety meds," said Geneva with clinical detachment.

"They found her lying under an overpass," added Iris, a little too loudly. "Coroner said there were enough drugs in her system to knock out a tiger. She must have stumbled and gone over the ledge."

"What was she doing walking along the overpass?" George asked.

No one could say.

"I spoke to Gerry about it," said Geneva, referring to her contact on the city police force. "It was the consensus of the precinct that there was nothing unusual about her death. Just one of those unfortunate things that happens from time to time. I lost an old student not too long ago—"

She paused, suddenly mindful of the murmur of chatter in the room around them. Investigating deaths for a living ought to have made her immune to their horrors, but she still found herself thinking of Brad at odd moments. "It would be a better world on all counts," she said, "if celebrity grifters hawking lousy advice were the biggest problems we had."

Iris gazed languidly down at the countertop. "I wonder if, maybe—"

But she never had the chance to finish her thought, for at that moment they heard a yell from near the entrance to the dining hall where two women stood circling each other combatively like a pair of disgruntled cats.

"I thought I asked you to leave me alone," said the first woman—the same who had been arguing with Mr. Koistinen when they entered the Hilton. "It's bad enough that you're constantly harassing me at work, but to follow me here—"

"It's a big event," said the other—a fit, muscular woman in forest-green camo pants and a black sleeveless shirt. "As a reporter, it's my job to be present at events of social and cultural interest—"

"That's total baloney and you know it, Serenity. You saw I was going into the bathroom and you stood outside waiting for twenty minutes until I came out—I'm sorry, can I help you?"

These words were addressed to a young man wearing a blue hoodie and a misshapen, strawberry-colored beanie who had appeared suddenly at her elbow carrying dozens of chocolate bars in wrappers in a little cardboard tray.

"Yeah." he said cheerfully. "We're selling chocolates to help cover the expenses for my aunt's funeral, and I was wondering if you might like to help out. These are some of the most nutritious chocolates on the market—they've got cherries, walnuts, Macadamia nuts..."

"Listen, I'm really sorry," said Serenity, "but we're kind of in the middle of something."

"Oh." said the man with a look of mild surprise. Recovering quickly, he added, "I'll just wait until you're finished."

And he continued to stand there, watching.

"Are they just going to keep arguing?" said Iris. "In the middle of a restaurant?"

"Maybe it's a performance," said Geneva. "I've seen this kind of thing before—actors staging fights to promote an upcoming play—"

"No, but I know that woman," said Iris. "The older one, I mean. Her name is Evelyn. She does fashion and obits for the *Beacon*."

"Who's the other?"

"No idea." Iris shrugged. "I get the feeling they're not on good terms, though."

"You don't say," said Geneva.

But no one intervened to break up the fight; no security guards appeared in the doorway; no uniformed staff materialized to implore them to calm down. The other patrons in the dining room, after waiting impatiently for a moment or two to see if the feud would escalate, had gone back to eating their meals and chatting when Evelyn said sharply, "If you come within thirty feet of me again, I'm filing a restraining order."

Serenity, oblivious to the man carrying the chocolate box and the stares of her fellow patrons, said, "That would put me in a difficult position, considering that we work in the same building."

"Rubbish," said Evelyn. "You don't come to work anymore. You sit at home in your pajamas and scroll Twitter."

"You spend half your time in the office doing the same thing," Serenity shot back, "so don't be getting all high and mighty."

"At least I put in the work," Evelyn replied. "People aren't begging Veronica to let me work from home because they can't stand being near me."

Serenity laughed oddly. "You've got a very skewed view of the situation if you think that's the reason she's had me working remotely—"

"It may surprise you to know that I see a lot of things you don't, Serenity," said Evelyn. "Believe it or not, I have a modicum of social awareness and don't go around acting like a catty middle-schooler."

"Um, if you don't mind my saying," said the man with the chocolate box, in a tone of excruciating politeness, "you're both being a little catty."

Serenity and Evelyn both turned to the man, blinking back surprise that he was still standing there. "No one asked you," they both said at once.

"And for your information," said Serenity, turning again to her foe, "using Twitter is part of my *job*. As a gossip columnist I would be out of work if I didn't have a means of collecting gossip."

"You don't vet your sources," cried Evelyn. "Twice now, we've had to retract published essays because they turned out to have been based on faulty information that you acquired from some anonymous bozo. The owner of a sports team is threatening to sue us for libel, so thanks very much for that."

"Every word I posted was true," said Serenity, surreptitiously creeping an inch or two closer to Evelyn. "Those people lied when they found out they were being quoted in the paper. They got cold feet and revoked their statements. Veronica knows this, which is the only reason I still have a job."

"You won't have one for much longer, if I have anything to say about it," said Evelyn in a low, dangerous tone. Stooping to retrieve her purse from the floor, she then rose and thrust a crooked finger in Serenity's face. "And if you threaten me again, if you threaten to murder me, if you so much as breathe a word about trying to silence me, the police will be beating down your door to drag you out of that smelly apartment."

Shoving past the man with the chocolate box, she stormed out of the dining hall and through the front doors before Serenity could put another word in.

Geneva rose at almost the same instant, looking somewhat perturbed, and tried to usher George and Iris toward the door. "Let's go, let's go," she said low, practically bouncing on her heels with impatience.

"Hang on, I haven't even finished my drink yet," cried George, bestowing an agonized look at his cup of fizzy soda.

"For heaven's sakes, just bring it with you. You can finish it in the car," said Geneva with uncharacteristic vehemence. "We need to get going."

"What's the hurry?" said Iris in a tone of alarm.

"I'll tell you in the car..." said Geneva in a sing-song voice.

The urgency of her manner plunged the rest of the group into mystery—mystery which deepened even further when a woman of about sixty, wearing a black leather jacket and a pair of ripped jeans, called out from the adjoining table and said, "No, don't worry about it. You can stay. I'm on my way out."

Geneva said not a word in acknowledgement; however, she did abruptly stop. George and Iris looked on in utter confusion as the woman threw away nearly a whole boat of fries and marched out of the dining hall.

"Yeesh, she had just sat down, too," said Iris. "Gen, did you know that woman? Gen?"

But Geneva didn't respond.

[6]

Monday morning brought a freak snowstorm which shut down the schools and rendered the major roads through Wrangler's Hill impassable. Iris awoke to an email from her boss informing her that the office was closed: "You can choose to work from home if you want, but honestly if I were you, I would take the day off." Iris did just this, spending much of the morning puttering about in the kitchen in her turquoise bathrobe and slippers making coffee and English muffins for herself and Geneva.

"George says he'll be coming over at around two or three if he can manage to shovel himself out of his driveway," said Geneva, seated at the kitchen table near the window with her laptop. "He's bringing hot chocolate and insisting that we watch 20,000 *Leagues Under the Sea*."

"The one with Kirk Douglas?" said Iris.

"Is there any other?"

Despite the promise she had made as they were leaving the Hilton on Saturday, Geneva still hadn't explained the identity of the mystery woman who had been seated next to them at dinner, nor why they had been so eager to get away from each other.

Iris waited until they were seated together at the table eating breakfast before once again broaching the subject. "What I want to know," she said, stabbing the air with a fork, "is why you've never mentioned this woman before."

Geneva set down her mug, and a little column of steam rose like a single tendril of white hair over the table. "I guess because it's never come up."

"Gen, I've known you for more than twenty years," Iris replied. "I know I'm not always the best judge of these things, but that woman hated you. If this is because of something that happened before I met you, how has she managed to hate you for this long?"

Geneva gritted her teeth in a pained expression, as if she would rather be talking about anything else. "Sometimes when we're young we develop these stupid rivalries," she said finally. "And then decades later we can't even remember why, or how they started."

If this answer was intended to satisfy Iris, it must have failed; for dunking a chunk of her muffin into the coffee, she said, "What's her name?"

"Joanne," said Geneva, practically spitting out the word. "Joanne Cowper—or at least, that was her name before. I have no idea whether she married or not."

"And is this rivalry, as you put it, entirely one-sided? Or do you hate her as much as she obviously hates you?"

Geneva blanched, as if not liking the framing of the question. "Old passions cool over the course of a few decades, or at least they're supposed to."

Iris raised a cool brow, as if to suggest that this hardly answered the question.

"Look, I don't know what else to tell you," said Geneva, throwing her spoon down. "We knew each other in high school. One of us did something to tick the other off; I can't even remember who started it at this point. I thought maybe she would've moved on by now, but apparently, she hasn't. I guess some people can carry petty grudges their whole lives."

"And you've just been spending the last twenty to thirty years not speaking to each other, avoiding each other at the supermarket...?"

Geneva shook her head. "She moved away shortly after graduation. This is the first time I've seen her in Lord knows how long. I guess something must have brought her back."

Perhaps sensing that it was best not to press the issue, Iris said no more, and they finished their breakfast in silence.

George arrived at the house around one, the shoulders of his coat covered in snow and a hardbound copy of *Twenty Thousand Leagues Under the Sea* under one arm, fairly buzzing about the wonders of aquatic life.

"I think this must be a different version from the one I read growing up," he said, "because there is a *lot* more detail about fish than I remembered." Here George opened the book and, pointing to a marked passage, said, "He mentions a fish known as a flycatcher that kills insects by shooting drops of water at them. The water strikes them at such high velocity that they fall from the air into the fish's waiting jaws."

"Think how useful that would be," said Geneva, shoving an egg and avocado salad in front of him. "We wouldn't even need to carry weapons."

George insisted on eating while they watched the movie, so he brought his bowl into the living room while Iris searched for it on streaming.

"Excited to watch this," said Geneva, who used to show it to her students on days when she was feeling sick and indisposed to teach, but they had only just reached the scene in which Ned sings, "Whale of a Tale" aboard the frigate, when her phone buzzed once in her purse. Keeping one eye on the screen, with a twinge of foreboding she pulled it out.

Gerry was texting. *Did you happen to run into Evelyn Rider at the Hilton on Saturday?*

I ran into someone named Evelyn, Geneva wrote back. *As I understand, she's a reporter for the Beacon. Why?*

("Gen, dear, put that away." said George.)

Gerry replied almost at once. *Evelyn seems to be missing. Nobody has seen her since that incident at the hotel on Saturday and her phone is going straight to voice mail. I'm trying not to expect the worst but... you know how these things go.*

Iris had turned round and was mumbling something, but Geneva couldn't hear. In the dim light, she looked rather like a fish opening and closing its mouth. Ignoring her, she said to Gerry, *Have you spoken to the other woman? The one who was berating her?*

To which Gerry replied, *Serenity's currently snowed in, but we zoomed with her briefly this morning. She doesn't have any idea where Evelyn went after that little tête-à-tête, as she drove straight home and has been shut in ever since. She's already facing an inquiry at work as a result of the events on Saturday. Did you happen to see what went on?*

I was there, said Geneva, *but I couldn't make heads nor tails of what they were fighting about. It looked like two women just screaming at each other. I got the impression that Evelyn felt as though Serenity had been stalking or harassing her.*

Yes, and she's not the first person to have made that complaint, said Gerry. *If it turns out that Evelyn came to some harm, it's going to look very bad for her.*

Surely you don't think it's as bad as that? said Geneva, remembering a previous instance in which someone who was thought to have been murdered was later revealed to be hiding in a tree house. *She might have gone out of town for the weekend.*

And not notified her employer or anyone else? said Gerry. *Gen, you have more faith in the people of this town than I do. It's getting to the point where if someone goes to the store and they're twenty minutes late getting back, I assume they were murdered.*

Maybe you should ask to be transferred, said Geneva.

Believe me, I've thought about it.

Iris and George were both scowling at her now. Geneva set her phone down on the coffee table where she could see if anyone texted and went back to watching the movie, though without much interest. Evelyn had only been gone for a day and a half, and there were any number of reasons she might have drifted out of contact. Geneva wasn't going to assume the worst until they had something more concrete than a sudden aversion to answering the phone.

The movie wore on. They had just reached the scene where Nemo, to the surprise and horror of his prisoners, rams a warship with the submarine when her phone buzzed again. This time she didn't recognize the number.

Hi, is this Geneva Pomolo? I got your number from your website. My name's Valerie Burnett. I recently bought a home in the Pine Crest subdivision and our first week the ceiling over the boys' bedroom collapsed. Thank God, they were staying over at a friends' house that night or it could have killed them. I spoke to a friend who's a builder and he said the room was built with concrete that had been mixed with some other, weaker substance in order to save money on construction. There's something really shady about this place. I worry that it's going to fall apart around us.

After reading this over a couple times, Geneva wrote back, *Valerie, I'm sorry to hear that. What do you want me to do about it?*

I'd like you to investigate the company that built this house, or the person who sold it to us. I think there's a good chance they're committing fraud, and I don't think we're the only people they've scammed.

Geneva took down the name of the realtor but warned Valerie that it might be two or three days before she was able to investigate properly. *I'll do what I can from home, but right now, I'm snowed in and there's a missing persons case that I'm about to be neck-deep in.*

Ah, well, nevertheless, said Valerie sadly. *Do let me know if you find anything.*

After the movie had finished, Iris hauled out the raspberry and peach pies that had been cooling in the fridge and began cutting them into slices, spraying every third slice with whipped cream. George stood rather uselessly at the head of the counter recounting some facts that he had learned from watching a documentary on the making of the movie.

"James Mason wasn't actually the first choice to play Nemo," he said. "He was brought onto the set at the last minute after someone else got sick and dropped out."

"George, dear, would you mind where you put your elbows?" said Iris, for George had nearly set his right elbow down in the whipped cream. "Personally, I prefer Ned over Nemo. I could stand on deck watching him sing, 'Whale of a Tale' till my legs gave out."

Iris shaved off the top of a pie slice with her finger and held it up to her lips. "What do you think, Gen? Would you rather be romanced by a hunky but dim sailor or a mad sea captain?"

Geneva had barely been paying attention. "I think we ought to get the driveway cleared out as soon as possible," she said, scratching the back of her neck absently. "They still haven't found Evelyn—oh, she's missing by the way, and I'm getting a little worried."

"What? That woman in the argument the other day? Missing? Well, that's for the police to handle," said Iris, not unreasonably. "Most people would see being snowed in as an opportunity to burrow in and not have to work for a day or two. You, you're just itching to get back out there on the road."

"I can't help it," said Geneva weakly. "People are in danger."

Iris waved a spoon covered in whipped cream in her direction. "That's the great thing about you," she said, "but even caring for others has its limits. You're only one person. You can't expect to save everyone."

George, meanwhile, had put on his boots and was already trudging dutifully toward the front door. "Georgie, where are you going?" Geneva asked.

"Figured I would do something to help out," George muttered, grabbing the shovel from its place by the door. "Shouldn't take more than twenty minutes, and I'll happily drive you wherever."

And he disappeared through the door into the swirling snow before they could utter a word of protest.

"I really thought we were going to get more than three consecutive days of spring weather," said Iris, gazing gloomily through the window as George shambled to the back of the driveway and began digging with the air of a miner in an underground tunnel.

"It's not technically spring for another two weeks," said Geneva, not that the distinction mattered this far north: one year it had snowed in the first week of May. "At least, the worst of winter is behind us."

"I wouldn't be too sure," said Iris, watching as the burden of snow sent a tree branch toppling to the ground below with a crack like thunder, where it narrowly missed hitting George.

"I'm starting to get why people retire to Florida," said Geneva, reaching for her phone, which had begun buzzing again.

"Personally, I wouldn't do Florida," said Iris with a look of visceral disdain, "though I've thought about moving back to South Carolina where I grew up. Winters are mild there and you only occasionally get a catastrophic, life-threatening hurricane. The crime rate isn't nearly as bad, either—so if you ever grow tired of saving people and decide you want to migrate to warmer climes, you could always come with me."

"I'm afraid we'll have to postpone our thoughts of retirement for another day," said Geneva, gazing unhappily at her phone. "It looks as though there may have been another murder."

Iris turned abruptly from the window. "What? Who?"

"Evelyn Rider," said Geneva with a miserable feeling. "They found her below the bridge—same bridge where that other woman's body was found just a couple months ago. I hate to say it, but it's starting to look as though we might be dealing with a serial murderer."

[7]

An hour later, Geneva and Iris were standing on the crest of the overpass which had been closed to through traffic. Snow was continuing to fall, thick and fast, and large flakes were accumulating on their coats and stinging their eyes and face. On the street below stood the coroner, wearing a white uniform that rendered her almost invisible against the backdrop of snow, directing the removal of the body into a depressingly cheery, canary-colored van.

Lieutenant Gerry Nelson had parked his car at the foot of the overpass and come trekking over on foot, clutching a bottle of anxiety meds in a plastic bag in the palm of one gloved hand.

"It's the same as the other woman," he said in a tone that evinced more anger than sorrow. "Overdosed on pills and tripped over the railing. Pathologist says, based on her preliminary survey of the body, that she must have died on impact. I don't for a minute think these two deaths are unconnected."

Geneva was inclined to agree, but she also wanted to be cautious. "Isn't it equally possible," she said, "that whoever committed this murder wanted us to *think* the two deaths were connected?"

"How do you figure?" said Iris.

"I mean, you've read your Agatha. Sometimes a murderer will try to conceal their motive by committing a copycat murder, designed to evoke the look of a previous killing in the hopes of misleading the police." Geneva raised an arm to her face to ward off the blinding snow. "If the same person had killed both of these women, I think he would try to make them *look* a little different. The fact that they're identical... well, it's almost as though he wants us to think he committed both murders."

Gerry had been making a valiant effort to follow Geneva's trail of thought but had gotten slightly irritated about halfway through.

"You remind me of that psychic I was interviewing on Friday," he said. He was kneeling now as if to survey the snowy asphalt. "Gen, these murderers aren't half as clever as you give them credit for. Sometimes a person just gets tired of another person's existence and wants to end them. No fuss, no strategies, no grand schemes, just a quick and not particularly well-planned death."

"You seem to know a lot about it," said Iris.

"I have to think about death a lot," Gerry replied.

They stood in silence for a moment, a silence punctured only by the persistent moaning of the wind. Some hundred yards away, a mile marker had come loose and was swinging from its hinge with a maddening creak like the sound of footsteps on an old staircase. Otherwise, the lack of traffic was unsettling: apart from the occasional eighteen-wheeler, there was hardly a car on the road. Geneva thought back to a homeless man she had spotted on the streets late in the summer, for whom she had offered to buy a sandwich at a local deli. She wondered where he resided now, and whether he had found shelter.

"Let's focus on this killing for the time being," said Geneva. "Whom do we know who might have wanted to kill her?"

"Besides the obvious, you mean?" Gerry stood to his feet. "Funnily enough, I had been compiling a list even before we found the body."

He reached into his coat pocket and produced a small yellow pad, which he flipped open toward the middle as he began to read. But he hadn't spoken more than a few words when there came a noise behind them of tires on ice and a black van pulled up to the bridge in almost the same spot where Gerry had parked his police car. As he and the two women looked on, a woman in a tight-fitting black cap and black windbreaker emerged with her hands raised. Geneva blanched and took a step or two backward; even from a distance of about forty feet she could see it was her old schoolmate, Joanne Cowper.

"I'm a reporter from the *Beacon*," said Joanne, after giving her name. "We were just informed that a body had been recovered from beneath this overpass—I was wondering if you might have any information on the victim, or how they died."

"You're not going to love this," said Gerry darkly. "It's the body of one of your fellow reporters."

Joanne's face turned an ashen color.

"Her name was Evelyn," said Geneva, choosing for the moment to put aside their longstanding grudge. "This is entirely off the record, but you can tell Veronica she appears to have been drugged and killed."

Ignoring Geneva as if she hadn't spoken, Joanne addressed herself to Gerry. "Who would want to do such a thing to poor Evelyn?"

"I was sort of hoping you would tell us," Gerry replied.

"I can only think of one person," said Joanne.

Geneva shook her head. "I'm not buying it. Hating someone doesn't automatically make them a killer, as you well know. Based on what I saw at the Hilton, it's obvious that Evelyn and Serenity weren't friendly, but I never got the impression that her life was in danger."

"Officer," said Joanne, still acting for all the world as though Geneva didn't exist, "it might interest you to know what Serenity said to Evelyn the last time she was in the office."

And she told them about the altercation in the editor's office, at the end of which Serenity had (allegedly) threatened to murder her.

"Evelyn was responsible for writing the *Beacon's* obituaries," said Joanne. "When Serenity told her, 'They'll be writing your obituary next,' we all understood what that meant. Serenity will deny that she meant anything of the kind, she'll claim that she was misheard, but we all heard it."

"Well, one way or another she seems to have gotten her wish," said Iris, glancing forlornly down at the nearly bare strip of road where the coroner's van had been parked only moments before. "I suppose it's possible that someone heard those threats and decided that now would be a good time to dispense of Ms. Evelyn, while the blame could be conveniently shouldered onto Serenity."

"My thoughts exactly," said Geneva. "It's what Agatha would've done."

"Guys, the murderer is not Agatha Christie," said Gerry in a tone of frustration. "Can we try to stay focused here, please?"

A sleek black bird flew through the snow overhead, looking stark against the pewter-gray sky. Geneva followed its descent for a moment in silence before adding, "You were going to share your list of suspects."

Gerry nodded. "I spent most of the morning compiling this list. When I spoke to Serenity over the internet—perhaps not the most reliable method but bear with me—she mentioned that Evelyn had reportedly been investigating a cluster of shoddily built houses in the West Wrangler's suburbs."

The mention of houses awoke something in Geneva's mind. "I just got a text about a badly built house," and she told them about the woman who had complained that a collapsing ceiling had nearly killed her two sons.

"Do you think the two things could be connected?" said Iris. "Maybe she nosed too close to a wide-ranging real estate scam."

"I'd like to put a name out there," said Joanne. The two women glanced up in surprise; she had been silent for so long that they had nearly forgotten she was there. "Last week Evelyn visited a professional psychic who's been the source of some very strange rumors of late."

"I've been seeing that woman's commercials on TV—if it's the same lady," said Iris. "There's a television in the office tuned to one of the local channels, and during the mornings, her ads play during *Matlock* and *Murder, She Wrote*. She wears a jeweled turban and talks in the most outrageously fake accent I've ever heard."

Geneva wanted to say something but had to wait until a soberingly large truck passed. "I'm sure she's a fraud, but I never got the impression she was trying to hide the fact. There's even a sign above the door to her shop saying, 'We're legally required to tell you that this is strictly for entertainment.' Granted, it's in very small letters..."

Joanne addressed her statement, though without ever looking at her directly. "Lately, Claudia has begun taking herself very seriously, by all accounts. She's been having what she's convinced are genuine visions and premonitions of future events. Evelyn spoke to her secretary and learned that she and Claudia were both baffled because this is the first time she's manifested anything like real psychic ability."

"That's a load of hogwash," said Gerry, hands now tucked firmly in the pockets of his coat. "She probably saw her client list beginning to dwindle and realized she needed to juice up her income by pretending to have had a conversion experience. So, she concocted a story where she went from being a fraud to being a real psychic."

The whole narrative surrounding Claudia struck Geneva as peculiar, though she couldn't say why yet. "Well, what have her customers been saying? What sort of experiences are they having?"

"That's why she's getting so much attention," said Iris, "because people are coming out of her sessions with the wildest stories. They say she'll leap up onto the table, appear to go into a trance for ten, fifteen minutes at a time, speak in foreign tongues, reveal information that the client had not told another living soul—"

"It's cold-reading," moaned Gerry, "this is textbook."

"Evelyn had come to the same conclusion," said Joanne, "which is why she went undercover to have her fortune read."

"And how did that go?" asked Iris.

Joanne had apparently decided that her longstanding feud with Geneva didn't extend to Geneva's partner. "Unfortunately, Claudia was on her best behavior. I think she may have known that Evelyn was a reporter for the paper, which —I guess is not exactly a secret."

"It sounds like maybe she has a database of everyone in Wrangler's Hill," said Geneva, "which wouldn't be that unusual. What I would like to know is why? What is her goal here? What does she think she's getting out of doing this whole song and dance?"

Joanne didn't have an answer to that, nor did anyone else.

"I think we had better pack this in soon," said Gerry, who was shifting his weight from side to side in the frigid air. "I'm starting to lose the feeling in both hands."

"I'm not done yet," said Iris, "I still have a lot of questions. Is the Steamy Bean open?"

"I don't think there's a single shop open within driving distance," said Geneva. On the drive over, they had passed mile after mile of empty parking lots and snow-blasted store fronts. "You're all welcome to come back to our house."

"I need to get going," said Joanne, a little too quickly. "I have another appointment."

"Fine," muttered Iris. "I didn't want you drinking all my ginger beer anyway." To Gerry she said, "Did Evelyn have any next of kin who need to be informed? Any sisters, a mother?"

Gerry bit down on his bloodless lip. "As it happens, her mother had only just died. I tried calling her this morning, thinking that maybe Evelyn had gone home for the weekend. She lived out in Washington State. Some woman answered. She said they had been expecting Evelyn to drive out next weekend and handle some legalities pertaining to the funeral; she was going to inherit a small sum of money."

"And they want us to believe she threw herself off a bridge?" said Iris.

Geneva said nothing. She had been keeping one eye all this while on Joanne, who now seemed in no hurry to leave. Gerry patted his pockets with a helpless gesture. "Well, unless there's anything else..."

"We should tell him," interjected Iris. "About the argument at the hotel."

"We've already talked about this," said Gerry, "I don't think—"

"No, not that one. The other one."

And together they told him about the disagreement they had overheard on their way up the stairs into the conference room, how someone working for Roman Koistinen had been badgering her into giving an introductory speech before Roman came out onstage.

"I wasn't following everything," said Geneva, "but it sounded as though he was trying to stiff her out of payment, and that this wasn't the first time he had done it."

"Sounds like more of a motive to kill Roman than to kill her," Gerry replied. "I'd like to talk to him, though, and find out whether that little tiff was ever resolved. He's from out of state, right? How long is he going to be in town?"

"I'll call the hotel tonight and find out," said Geneva, relieved at having a direction. "It's entirely possible he was planning to jet and got snowed in by the blizzard. In which case, I don't think we'll have too much trouble finding him."

"You do that," said Gerry, tugging his hat down over his ears and beginning to slink away in the direction of his car. "I'm going to head back to the station and call this woman's aunt and let her know we found her." He didn't sound as though he particularly relished the prospect.

After he had gone, there was an awkward moment in which Iris, Geneva, and Joanne continued to stand silently together. Then, without so much as a word of farewell, Joanne turned sharply on her heels and began to walk back across the overpass.

Sensing that the opportunity to talk was quickly fading, Geneva called after her, "Joanne? Joanne, if you'd wait just a second—"

But it was no use. Joanne accelerated her pace as she hurried back to the van, coat drawn over her shoulders, against the wind.

[8]

WHEN THEY REACHED HOME that evening, they found George seated on the sofa still thoroughly absorbed in reading *Twenty Thousand Leagues Under the Sea.*

"Right now, they're tearing through the Mediterranean," he said, "and Ned wants to escape to Italy, so Nemo steers the *Nautilus* through boiling water." He cackled with malicious glee; then, seeing the gloomy looks on their faces, added, "I don't suppose you managed to catch the murderer in the hour you were gone?"

"No murderers caught," said Geneva, "though we've got about a dozen people who might have wanted to kill this pretty inoffensive and dull woman." She strode into the kitchen, where Iris was trying to decide whether to make pot-stickers or spaghetti with meatballs for dinner, and pulled out her phone. "Fingers crossed that Mr. Koistinen doesn't give us the run-around."

She dialed the front desk of the hotel, where, after explaining that she was conducting a criminal investigation and that it was a matter of some urgency, she was patched through to Mr. Koistinen's room. An unfamiliar voice answered. "Vince Overton speaking," he said, "may I ask who's calling?"

"They must have given me the wrong number," said Geneva. "I'm looking for a Mr. Roman Koistinen."

"This is his personal secretary," said Mr. Overton. After a short pause, during which Geneva thought she could hear much whispering and hissing, he added, "Mr. Koistinen isn't here at the moment, he went out to get wine and chips—"

"In a snowstorm?" said Geneva, before she could prevent herself.

"It's remarkably good wine," Mr. Overton replied. There came a noise as of someone drumming on a desktop. "I can leave a message for when he gets back."

Geneva was prepared to let him go, but then a new idea occurred to her. "Say, I think I ran into you the other night at the conference. You were on the stairs having a discussion with someone... a journalist."

From the noise of the bedsprings, Geneva inferred that he was shifting uncomfortably. "Just a contract negotiation with one of our employees... She's something of an established author herself, and we were hoping she might warm up the crowd."

"It might interest you to know that the woman in question is dead," said Geneva (ignoring Iris, who was attempting to get her attention by waving a bag of frozen shrimp in one hand and a bag of frozen taquitos in the other). She heard what sounded like a faint gasp on the other end, then more muttering. "Her body was found beneath an overpass near Wernall not more than a couple hours ago. We believe she may have taken her own life."

Hearing this admission, Mr. Overton seemed to lower his guard a little. "This is a really horrible coincidence," he said, "because she's the second woman of my acquaintance to have taken her life since the new year."

"Is that right?" said Geneva, attempting sympathy but mostly sounding morbidly curious.

"I had an old school friend, Madeline," he went on quietly. "I'm sure you heard about it. It was all over the news."

"I knew she had died, yes." She waited a beat before adding, "When do you think Mr. Koistinen will be back?"

After an interminable pause, Mr. Overton said, "He won't be coming back at all tonight."

"Mr. Overton," said Geneva, "how long does it take to run to the store?"

"Hey, there's a big storm," replied Mr. Overton. "It's bad."

He hung up before she could mount a rebuttal.

Swearing under her breath, Geneva reached for her coat and purse. Iris, who was heating up a bag of frozen carrots in a pan of melted butter, watched her heading toward the door with a bemused expression.

"Hang on, where are you going?" said George, glancing up from his book.

"George, don't try to cook, we'll bring you something back," said Geneva. She opened the door and a blast of late-winter wind hit her full in the face. "Iris and I have an appointment."

Iris turned off the stove and grabbed for her boots under the table. "Appointment for what?" she asked.

"To meet Roman Koistinen." said Geneva, who was already halfway out the door.

———

"I don't know if you've been following this story," said Iris as they tore through the deserted streets with snowbanks piled high on either side like canyon walls, "but Robert Wheelwright, who runs the Double Bubble Soda Company, was just on TV saying someone is trying to blackmail him."

"Who?"

"That's the thing, he doesn't have any clue. He says he received an anonymous note claiming that the sender had incriminating video footage and was threatening to post it unless their demands were met. He decided to come forward to get ahead of the story."

"What was on the videos? What are they accusing him of doing?"

They were approaching an intersection with a flashing red light. Seeing that there were no other cars in the vicinity, Iris sped through it without even slowing down—a bit risky considering the weather conditions. "Apparently he had... *hired* a woman to escort him to the premiere of a play at the Mozz."

"Hired? What do you mean, hired?"

"I'll leave you to draw your own conclusions," said Iris, honking at a flock of blackbirds that were pecking around at some carcass in the middle of the street. The birds scattered and reconvened atop an icy power line. "His wife died a while back, and I'm guessing he was probably lonely and wanted to experience the joy of dating again. Still, pretty embarrassing."

"What's embarrassing is that he couldn't find a date without paying for it," said Geneva.

"The point is, though," said Iris, as they pulled once more into the parking lot of the hotel, "someone is calling up the richest people in this town and trying to squeeze money out of them by threatening to expose their most mortifying secrets."

"A real estate scam, a melodramatic psychic, two murders and now a scheme to shake down the rich," said Geneva, unbuckling her seat belt. "When do these people find time to sleep?"

The clerk at the front desk refused to give them the number of the room in which Overton and Koistinen were staying but offered to call them and inform them that there were guests in the lobby who wanted to meet them. Somewhat to Geneva's surprise, Mr. Overton invited them up. They found him standing in the door of a room on the fourth floor, a beefy man with a broad, flabby face like a flank of mutton whose bulk so filled the doorway that they couldn't see past it.

"You're not interrupting anything," he said, "I was just making a spreadsheet listing all my bootleg VHS tapes from 1995 to 2002 inclusive—"

"No offense to you, Mr. Overton," said Geneva, "but we were rather hoping we could speak to your boss." As she said this, there came a crash from the room behind him, followed by muffled swearing.

"I already told you he won't be back tonight," said Mr. Overton, agitation shining on his red face, "he's—"

"Gone out through the window?" guessed Iris.

"Yeah," Mr. Overton said with a resigned shrug.

Iris took the elevator back down to the ground floor while Geneva pushed past Mr. Overton, who didn't offer up much resistance. The window at the back of the room stood open and feathery flakes of snow were drifting into the room, forming a powdery carpet. She glanced down in time to see the curled, bobbing head of Mr. Koistinen emerging from the fire escape. He wasn't wearing a coat—there had been no time to grab one when he learned that the girls were on their way—and he winced in regret as the knife-like wind tore into his body.

"Mr. Koistinen," Geneva called after him, "you're a fool if you think you can get away from me that easily."

"Watch me!" said Mr. Koistinen, tearing across the parking lot on his slender legs (the way he ran put Geneva in mind of a chicken strutting across the floor of a barn). He was so keen to get away that he nearly ran headlong into a passing van, and by the time he had apologized to the driver, who had stopped and was yelling at him, Iris was waiting for him on the other side of it like an inescapable specter.

Seeing her standing there, Mr. Koistinen flung up his hands in a gesture of despair and allowed himself to be marched back into the hotel.

"I'll be honest," said Mr. Koistinen, once they were gathered back in his room and the window closed, "I'm somewhat of a fraud. Is that why you're chasing me? All right. I confess. I don't know the first thing about writing."

"But those books," said Iris, aghast. "All your practical advice—"

"Purely a way of making money, I'm afraid." He had the grace to look more than a little ashamed. "Oh, I wanted to be a writer. I wanted to tell the greatest stories the world had ever seen. From the ages of eleven to thirty-two, I poured my heart into writing fiction, penning wonderful pastiches of all my favorite books I had read growing up— Verne, Bradbury, Dickens, you name it. I wrote marvelous tales of submarine voyages and travels inside the human body and little girls having adventures underground. I compiled some of my best work and sent it off to an agent and you know what they told me?"

"What?" asked Iris and Geneva together.

"Rubbish!" cried Mr. Koistinen in a severe tone. "Complete and utter rubbish, the lot of it. Oh, I could mimic the masters—a parrot or a trained monkey could have done that—but in all those millions of words, in all those dozens of novels and hundreds of novellas, there was not a single original idea, a single character who imprinted herself on the memory, a single lingering image. Not a single moment in all that dreck that could comfort or move or inspire. They tell you that you need only ten thousand hours of practice to become a master in your field, but they lie. By the age of thirty-two, I was staring down the awful possibility that I lacked genius. Talent I had a-plenty, but not the creative spark that brings a book to life."

Given the man's eloquence, Geneva was inclined to doubt that his work was as bad as he claimed. "So you got one rejection," she said. "Surely another agent—"

"I mailed or emailed, phoned and cajoled every agent in New York City and the greater New York area," said Mr. Koistinen. "Again and again, the verdict was returned, stamped in red letters: Failure. Derivative. A total hack. No, I'm afraid at this point, there's no improving. At some point, you simply have to cut your losses and find some productive trade in which to while away your waking hours."

They had drifted somewhat from the main reason for their visit. Clearing her throat apologetically, Geneva said, "I understand that you and Evelyn had a row on Saturday last."

Mr. Koistinen grimaced uncomfortably, scratching at his neck. "I've got nothing to hide anymore," he said. "I didn't kill her, if that's what you're thinking—"

"No one said you did," said Geneva.

Unexpectedly, Mr. Overton spoke up from the corner of the room. "Tell them about your financial troubles."

Mr. Koistinen shot him an accusing glare but nodded in acquiescence. "Sales of my last few books have not been spectacular," he said. "And I... well, I made some unwise investment decisions—"

"Gambling," said Mr. Overton.

"Thank you, Vince," said Mr. Koistinen. "Anyway, so much depended on this weekend's symposium. I was hoping to make a bundle with the number of people who had signed up to hear my lectures. There were several other people scheduled to speak on the roster, but all of them backed out when they learned they weren't going to be compensated. Evelyn was particularly upset about it."

"As I recall," said Mr. Overton, "she said she was going to leave the imprint of her high heel on the back of your skull."

"Not one of my proudest moments." Mr. Koistinen unwrapped a mint chocolate in a green wrapper and sucked on it pensively. "And of course, when she backed out, I had to fill in for her, and for all the others, which meant I ended up having to do five lectures in a single weekend. You can bet I wasn't happy about it, but murder?" He shuddered, like someone biting down on an anchovy when they had been expecting pineapple. "Murder doesn't solve problems. It only creates more problems."

"Too right," said Geneva. "But I can tell you the police aren't going to be sympathetic. You were seen quarreling with a woman on Saturday, and she was found dead two days later."

"Yes, and I wasn't the only one," said Mr. Koistinen, with renewed energy. "That other woman, what's-her-name... the way they were going at it, I thought they were going to murder each other right then and there." He laughed mechanically. "Save me the trouble of having to do it."

Seeing the look on the women's faces, he added, "I didn't mean that. I don't mean that."

"Did you threaten Evelyn in any way?" asked Iris.

"I'm sure I said a lot of things I'm not proud of," said Mr. Koistinen evasively. "I can be very persuasive when I need to be."

"Clearly," said Geneva. "That's why all of your guest lecturers backed out."

"Well..." He stared miserably down into the bottom of his soda. "Like I said, words have only gotten me so far in life."

Sensing that they had extracted from Mr. Koistinen all that they were going to get, Geneva turned to his secretary, who had returned to his desk and was now busily editing some grainy video footage. "I don't suppose you can vouch for all of Mr. Koistinen's movements over the past forty-eight hours?"

"He disappeared for about five hours yesterday," said Mr. Overton cheerfully. "He still won't tell me where he went."

"Hey, you're fired," said Mr. Koistinen in a very matter-of-fact tone.

Mr. Overton merely shrugged. "Good luck finding another secretary who will consent to the wages you pay me," he said, and went on editing his video as though nothing had happened.

Geneva and Iris bade the two men farewell and took the elevator back down to the lobby. Geneva was mostly silent on the way home, pondering the pitiful figure of Mr.

Koistinen as she gazed through the window at the frozen, marbled waters of Lake Alpaca.

"You almost feel sorry for the guy," said Iris as she pulled onto their street. "All those years wasted, thinking he was some kind of genius. Almost makes me want to retire my pen and forget that I ever wanted to become an author."

"That's the trouble with this country, isn't it?" said Geneva sadly. "Everybody thinks they're some kind of genius."

[9]

On Thursday when the weather cleared, George drove Geneva down to the police station to meet with Gerry. He had not been idle during the blizzard: he had spent much of the week compiling Madeline Ponderphelt's extant correspondence gathered from different sources—her kin and friends mainly, which he placed into a shoe box and handed over to Geneva when she reached the station.

"I haven't yet had time to read through all of it," he said. "Gomez is breathing down my neck to stay focused on the Rider case and stop digging into old cases. I'm having the hardest time in the world trying to convince them the two could be connected. In their world, if a woman has been dead for more than three weeks she's already passed out of memory."

"I'll go through them," said Geneva, opening the lid of the box and peering inside. It was crammed full of letter after letter written in Madeline's pinched, indecipherable handwriting. She felt as though she had been given a set of old Dwarfish runes to translate.

She spent much of the afternoon and late into the evening sitting at the kitchen table reading through the letters, occasionally pausing to type up a stray line or paragraph that might prove pertinent to the case. When Iris arrived home at half past five wearing a distractingly large hat in the shape of a chicken (she claimed to have won it in a raffle), Geneva summarized her findings.

"This might end up being nothing," she said, removing her glasses and rubbing her tired eyes, "but Madeline typically signed her correspondence 'Maddie,' even when writing letters of a professional nature. It seems this is the name she preferred for herself. But I looked up a PDF of the suicide note online and she signed it 'Madeline.' Really makes you wonder."

Iris, who had been strutting around the kitchen peering at her own reflection in the door of the microwave, frowned skeptically. "I wouldn't say it necessarily proves anything. She might have been in a state of mental duress when she wrote the letter. I mean, she was obviously under mental duress if she took her own life."

"That's what I thought at first," said Geneva, who had been anticipating this objection. "But then I came across some letters she had written in 2012, right after Mandara, her teenage daughter, was struck down and killed by a drunk driver while walking home from a New Year's Eve party. The letters are barely coherent—Madeline seems to have been out of her mind with grief—but she still signed them 'Maddie.'"

Iris nodded, looking impressed, and the chicken atop her head bobbed up and down. "Well, I guess that settles it. What else have you got?"

"There was one other thing," said Geneva, with all the fervor of an archeologist sifting through old bones. "I don't know if Gerry has read this, but there's a typewritten, printed-out letter that's full of insinuations and veiled threats." She pulled out the letter and began to read: "Madeline: you might think it's cute to threaten someone in this way, but I find it neither cute nor funny. I don't think you're fully aware how nasty I can get when I have my back against the wall, and you had better hope you never find out."

"Sounds menacing," said Iris, trotting over and reading the note over her shoulder. "I don't suppose we have any way of knowing who might have written it?"

"No, but I have my suspicions." Geneva folded the note and set it back into the box. "Who do we know with a habit of threatening others when she doesn't get her way?"

"Half the ladies in the Gardening Club," said Iris, who was still salty about having been thrown out.

"Besides that."

"Oh, that reporter, what's her name... Serenity."

Geneva nodded. "After dinner I think we'll need to drive down to her apartment and find out what motivated this letter."

"I certainly never wrote a letter of that nature, nor would I have any reason to," said Serenity as they stood in her apartment an hour later. Behind her through the windows, the sun was slowly setting over the high-rise, bathing the parking lot in dusky gold and burnt orange.

"Why would I go to the trouble of bothering a middle-aged woman who was clearly distraught after the untimely death of her daughter? I resent the insinuation."

"Because it wouldn't be the first time you've berated and threatened a middle-aged woman," said Geneva in a prickly tone. "On the way over I did a quick Google search and learned that you were arrested for drunken and disorderly conduct at the age of twenty-two. Would you care to explain what that's about?"

Serenity made a calculating expression, as if wondering how deceptive she could be and get away with it.

"Well, I don't suppose there's any point in withholding the truth," she said after a long pause. "I was *arrested* at a public demonstration, *allegedly* for punching a bystander who happened to be taking photographs. I'm using scare-quotes to underscore that I was never actually charged with a crime, and the jury declared me not guilty."

"Were you guilty?" asked Iris.

"Not legally," said Serenity, somewhat evasively. "Anyway, I'm thirty-four now, and this is all ancient history. You can't plausibly argue that I murdered a couple of defense-less old women just because I may or may not have gotten physical with a protester back when MTV still played music."

"No one is accusing you of being a murderer," said Geneva, feeling a little exasperated. "But I would like to know where you were between Saturday evening, when you left the hotel, and Monday afternoon when Evelyn's body was discovered."

"Do you want me to draw you a *chart?*" asked Serenity angrily; then adding a little more quietly, "I'm sorry. Where would you like me to start?"

"How about with where you went on Saturday night?" said Iris. Geneva nodded.

"After I left the hotel, I drove over to the *Beacon* and spent about an hour trying to get inside to retrieve some pictures I had taken at Madeline's funeral."

Serenity rose and strode into the kitchen, where she poured herself a glass of water and stirred a lemon into it. She didn't ask the two women whether they wanted anything. "The building was locked, and I think the locks must have all recently been changed, because my key—the key that they gave me when I got the job—no longer worked. There's a window at the back of the building that's usually unlocked, and once when I forgot my key at home, I managed to climb through it, but no such luck this time."

"Did you go back on the next day?" asked Iris, eyeing the water unhappily.

"Sunday morning," said Serenity, "I spent following up another lead. I'd learned through the Slack channel that Evelyn had been investigating an anonymous tip—that someone in Wrangler's Hill is selling shoddily built houses at mark-down prices.

"Wanting to get the jump on Evelyn, I did some digging of my own, and it led me to a realtor named Dinah—Dinah Whistledown. I drove over to her house and caught her just as she was heading out the door on the way to church. As you can imagine, she wasn't too happy to see me. I pointed out that she had been linked back to four different houses that had collapsed in whole or part with families living inside them and asked if she held herself to blame for that. Dinah said, 'I have no idea what you're talking about' and threatened to call the police and report me for stalking and harassment."

"Dinah Whistledown," said Geneva, writing the name in her notepad. "I'd like to speak with her. Maybe we'll have better luck."

"She's an ornery cuss," said Serenity, fishing the lemon out of the glass and squeezing what juice remained into her mouth. "At one point, she slapped herself with her purse and warned me that if I came any closer, she would tell the police I had hit her. I felt no inclination to stick around after that."

Geneva was inclined to wonder why Serenity seemed to be a magnet for drama. "And you think you could prove this woman has been engaged in real estate fraud?"

"Someone is," said Serenity, "and I would consider her the most likely culprit. She's also sold something like twenty houses in the past week, and I would like to know how she's done it. You could argue that she's simply a very talented saleswoman, but no one is that talented." She frowned thoughtfully, which had the effect of making her nose seem abnormally large. "There's something fishy about it, or my name isn't Serenity Sparklan."

Geneva was beginning to wonder if perhaps she had misjudged Serenity. Certainly, she was brash and immature and temperamental, but it was precisely those qualities that might make her a good reporter if she ever learned to manage herself. She reminded Geneva of Iris, somehow—both of them forever landing themselves in trouble by speaking their minds and asking too many questions.

"Serenity, I did a little bit of background investigating prior to coming over," said Iris, "and it seems you left your last job in Columbus very suddenly. What was that about?"

Serenity looked as though she would rather not talk about it.

"They let me go," she said after a hesitation, "because I had sent some emails to a source trying to get her on the record, and the woman went and took her own life in the middle of the banana bread aisle of a bakery. Got blood all over the banana bread. So the editor-in-chief blamed *me*, because they said I had 'bullied her into doing it.' Which was a lot of nonsense, frankly."

She shook her head in derision, as if she had been the person chiefly injured by the woman's death.

"I'm not accusing you," said Geneva, "but you have been linked to a disturbing number of deaths. Where did you go on Sunday after you confronted this woman Dinah?"

"I drove over to Beech Grove," said Serenity, "to visit my friend Lorina Collins-Lighthouse. She'd recently suffered a miscarriage and needed some girl time. We spent the afternoon eating pizza bagel bites and watching *Lord of the Rings: The Fellowship of the Ring*, and then, because it was getting late, she asked if I wanted to spend the night. I didn't get home until dusk on the following day, which is when I learned they had recovered Evelyn's body."

Iris was doing some quick mental calculations. "You drove back to Wrangler's Hill in the middle of a snowstorm?" she said.

"I didn't want to overstay my welcome," Serenity replied—which was perhaps the most unconvincing thing she had said so far.

"Can we verify this?" said Geneva. "Is there a way we can get hold of this… Lorena Lighthouse, is it?"

"Lorina Collins-Lighthouse," said Serenity. "And I can call her if you'd like."

"No, I think we had better call her," said Geneva, who had read several Agatha Christies in which criminals manage to convey to associates that they need to lie about an alibi. "Would you mind sharing her number?"

Reluctantly, Serenity brought up the contacts on her phone and rattled off a string of numbers. Geneva rang the woman up and they waited. Soon a voice came over the speaker saying the number had been disconnected.

"Sounds like she might have forgotten to pay her phone bill," said Geneva, taking note of Serenity's visible discomfort. "Are you sure that's the right number?"

"Of course, it's the right number, I checked and double-checked." Serenity's face turned an unsightly purplish color, as if a noose were being drawn around her neck. "Call her again in an hour and maybe she'll pick up. We spent the whole weekend together."

"Can anyone else vouch for you?"

"No, because no one else was with us." There was a note of pleading in Serenity's voice now. "I'll email her. I'll send her a text. I promise I wasn't anywhere near here when Evelyn was murdered. We might have hated each other, but I wouldn't kill her. What would that accomplish?"

[10]

By the time they left the apartment, night was falling; the sky was impossibly blue, as if the houses and town had sunk to the bottom of the sea. The temperature had fallen by another ten degrees while they were interviewing Serenity, and Geneva nearly slipped coming down the stairs on a particularly slick patch of ice. She might have fallen, too, if Iris had not instinctively reached out a hand and caught her.

"Home?" said Iris as they shambled toward the car, hugging themselves tightly.

"I promised George we'd bring him some food," said Geneva, "but before we head home, there's one more stop I'd like to make." Opening her phone, she read out the address and Iris typed it into the GPS. Behind them, they could see Serenity starting her car and beginning to pull out of the driveway. "I wonder where she's going at this hour."

"Gen, I'm not even sure where *we're* going," said Iris.

"I'd like to meet this realtor," Geneva replied. "The one who was giving Evelyn such trouble."

The realtor's house lay on the other side of town, in an upper-class neighborhood of a gated golf course, landscaped parks, and stately three-story homes that would have made a medieval king envious. They passed the front of a night club where three men wearing royal blue tailored suits were just emerging from the back of a limousine, the youngest of the three making an ill-conceived attempt to freestyle rap while his two companions tried hard not to laugh.

Geneva lapsed into silence, absorbed in thoughts of who might have written Madeline's final note. Iris, who had been singing along to "You Keep Me Hangin' On" by the Supremes, suddenly turned down the radio and said, "We've got about ten minutes. Why don't you tell me what's going on between you and Joanne?"

"Iris, I already told you—"

"And I'm not an idiot. I can tell when you're not giving me the full truth. So let's have it out, now."

Geneva let out an unhappy sigh. "Maybe if I tell you, I can stop thinking about it. My junior year of high school, Joanne and I were both running to be editor of the school newspaper the following year. I had never cared for her much because she was abrasive and domineering, always sticking her nose in other people's business. I was more relaxed, professional, had a good rapport with our teacher and the rest of the staff."

Geneva winced as she thought back to the events of more than thirty years ago. "Everyone said I was a shoo-in, but I didn't feel very confident. Then I overheard Mrs. Reese-Holland telling someone privately that she was seriously considering giving the position to Joanne because her work that year had been outstanding. Of course, being seventeen and angry, I saw it differently. Joanne had been kissing up to her the whole year, angling for the position." Geneva adjusted the hot air vent so that the hot air was blowing on her. "I don't know what I was thinking, I didn't even really want the position as much as she did…"

"So what happened?" asked Iris.

"I wrote an anonymous letter to the editor, disparaging Joanne's character in the most maligning terms. I said she was a plagiarist, a cheater and a bad kisser. I said she had been seen making out with two boys on the same day, which was true—although I left out that she had been trying to get information from both of them for a story. I said she had been the one who had planted a stink bomb in Principal Cranmer's office so that she could sneak in there and steal some important files. Nothing I said was a lie, exactly, but I still shouldn't have snitched.

"When Mrs. Reese-Holland read the letter, she was appalled. She had a private chat with Joanne that lasted for hours, at the end of which she decided that Joanne shouldn't be in charge of running the paper. I had covered my tracks well enough that it wasn't clear I had sent the letter, and most people didn't suspect me because I had a reputation for being such a sweet, friendly person. Joanne knew, though. She confronted me after the meeting and said, 'You're probably going to get the editor job, but you and I both know how you got it, and I will never forgive, or forget it.' That was the last thing she ever said to me. She didn't speak to me at all the next year, not even once, even though we were both on staff."

"Did you get the position?" asked Iris.

"I did," said Geneva slowly. "Though I rather wished I hadn't. Joanne was a little obnoxious, but we had been friends before. I just wanted the gig so badly—wanted it because she wanted it, because I knew she was going to get it—and then when I got it, I realized I didn't want it nearly as much as I thought I did. I considered resigning and yielding the position over to her, but I knew Mrs. Reese-Holland wouldn't let me. I had already burned that bridge. I'd burned a lot of bridges."

By now, they had pulled up outside of the house which the GPS had indicated as Dinah's. Because there were two cars in the driveway, Iris parked along the curb, in front of an inflatable nativity scene depicting characters from various Christmas movies—George Bailey, Kevin McAllister, John McLane, the Grinch—gathered around a crèche ("a little blasphemous, but okay," Geneva sniffed as they made their way to the door).

"Not to mention it's past Valentine's Day," said Iris as she rang the doorbell.

The door opened a crack and a woman peered out, her frizzy hair knotted up in a loose bun, looking oddly like a turtle emerging from its carapace. "I'm sorry, do I know you?"

"We're looking for a Ms. Dinah Whistledown?" said Geneva.

"Speaking," said Dinah, "but if you're with those religious fanatics who came by earlier—"

"We're assisting the local police," Geneva replied.

Dinah looked briefly crestfallen. She opened the door more widely. "Assisting? In what capacity?"

"Just asking questions. I understand that you met with a reporter for the *Beacon* just a few days before her body was found under the Overpass over by the Dairy Queen off Highway 41."

Dinah knitted her brows in surprise. "You mean that brazen hussy? I won't pretend I liked her much, but for you to insinuate—"

At that moment, however, she was cut short by a most unlikely interruption. The door leading into the dining room swung open and a woman strode into the living room, carrying a wedge of Brie cheese in one hand. Although she was wearing neither turban nor feathers, she was, unmistakably, the woman they had both seen on TV.

"So I'm trying this new thing," said Claudia, "where I try a bite of the cheese and then a bite of the almond, and let me tell you—" She paused in mid-stride as she saw the two women standing in the doorway. "Oh. Hello."

"Claudia?" said Geneva with a surreal feeling, as if the Doctor from *Doctor Who* had just wandered into the room.

"I'm sorry, do you two know each other?" Dinah asked.

Iris, however, was one or two steps ahead of her. "Call me a dummy—in fact, I must be a dummy, because it never occurred to me to wonder if Claudia had a surname."

Dinah wheeled round and shot Claudia a venomous glare, as if to signal for silence; but Claudia, evidently not taking the hint, said, "Oh, it's Whistledown, same as everyone else in our family. Even if I got married, I probably wouldn't change it. I'm too much of a feminist."

Geneva was beginning to see what Iris was getting at. To the great consternation of Dinah, whose face had turned a horrible plum color, she said, "This certainly puts some things in perspective, wouldn't you say?"

"I'm not receiving any visitors at this hour," Dinah cried, and attempted to close the door; but Iris flung a deft foot in her way and said to her partner:

"You mean how that old fraud back there has been recruiting people for her sister's business? Yes, I'd say it certainly does."

"I'm sure you're both talking nonsense," said Dinah, still scowling at her sister as she kicked at Iris's foot, "and if you don't leave my property this instant, I'll be forced to call the police."

"Please do," said Geneva in a relaxed tone. "I seem to recall several of your venerable sister's customers reporting that she spoke to them in a guttural tone, claimed that she was receiving visitations from their dead loved ones, and that these loved ones had told them to move out of their houses immediately because they were in terrible danger."

"Yes, and what of it?" said Claudia, indignantly waving the Brie round. "You can't question a person's psychic gift."

"So what we can safely assume must have happened," said Iris, "is that these grief-stricken, frightened people, having lost the most precious members of their families and now being without a home—"

"Be quiet," cried Dinah, reaching for her purse which was hanging on a coatrack beside the door and beginning to hit them with it, though without much effect. "I demand that you cease this irritating prattle."

"... Claudia, being the dear and loving sister that she is," said Geneva, looking amused by the whole scene, and paying no more attention to Dinah's abuses than if she were a gnat, "sent those grieving, vulnerable customers straight into the arms of Dinah Whistledown, realtor... whom they did not know was the elder sister of one Claudia Whistledown, otherwise known as the Incredible Claudia."

"What do you want me to say?" said Dinah nastily. "You're both very smart. I wish you would both retire to Florida and leave the rest of us to live in peace."

"Not while there are still criminals to be antagonized, my dear Dinah," said Iris. "You're digging your own grave selling people those collapsible houses. So far, you've been very lucky, but the second a piece of masonry or a roof beam falls on some poor woman's kid, you'll be pining for the days when we came by and harassed you. It won't be hard to prove that you knew about the shoddiness of all those houses."

"You aren't getting another word out of me," said Dinah, who had finally managed to prod Iris out of the doorway. "Go home and watch *Matlock*."

"I prefer *Murder, She Wrote*, for your information," said Geneva, reaching for her phone which had begun to buzz.

"Maybe if you'd watched some of those old shows growing up," added Iris, looking distinctly ruffled at having been forced out, "you would have thought twice before leading a life of *crime*."

Dinah slammed the door. From within, they could hear the bolts being drawn and then, a second later, the living room blinds being closed.

"Well, I don't know how much that accomplished," said Iris, glowering at the front door with the Christmas wreath still hanging on it, "but it was certainly satisfying." Turning to Geneva she added, "Home, then?"

"I'm afraid not yet," said Geneva, who was giving her phone a look such as Iris had seen only one or two times before. "There's still one more stop we have to make. And I think we had better call the police while we're at it."

She passed the phone to Iris, who read the message indicated:

Geneva? This is Serenity. I tried calling the local PD and they're not answering. I'm down at the Beacon's offices, fourth floor, hiding in a closet. Everyone else is gone for the night. There's someone at my computer trying to guess my password. They've got a huge knife, and I think they're going to kill me.

[11]

"What do you suppose they're looking for on her computer?" asked Iris as they sped down the highway, going just under the speed limit. In places, the roads were still icy, and once or twice the car nearly skidded.

"I've got a few theories," said Geneva, holding fast to the arm grip. "Serenity mentioned that she was trying to get some files off of her computer, but that she was having trouble getting into the office."

"Sure, but why would someone else want them? Want them enough to break into the building in the dead of night, no less?"

Geneva didn't have a good answer for this. Nor did she have any real plan for saving Serenity, beyond rushing headlong into danger and hoping the police arrived in time to save them from being murdered. "You know you don't have to do this, right?" said Iris. "We could just wait until they get here."

But the note of resignation in her voice suggested that she already knew it was hopeless. "He doesn't appear to be carrying any weapons," said Geneva, "apart from the one knife—"

"That we know of," said Iris.

Geneva feigned deafness. "We might even be able to scare him into surrendering that. Anyway, I'm worried. Worried about Serenity. Worried that he might find her before the police can get there."

Iris parked the car in the parking lot of a McDonald's across the street from the *Beacon* and dutifully followed Geneva toward the front entrance, who seemed to be calculating that she would be going in one way or another and would be more likely to survive the journey if Iris went with her.

Mounting the steps slowly, so as not to slip, Geneva reached the door and jiggled the handle. Locked. She swore under her breath.

"How are we supposed to get in?" said Iris.

"Probably the same way *he* did," said Geneva, gingerly brushing past her. "The back window."

They trotted around the side of the building, a distance of about sixty paces, to a back entrance standing atop a small flight of stairs. To the right, above a clump of frost-rimed bushes, stood an open window. It was just low enough that Geneva thought she could clamber through into the dim interior, but Iris paused with a hesitant look on her face.

"I'm sorry," she said, "I don't know if you've noticed but I'm a little bit thicker around the middle than you are."

"What are you getting at?" said Geneva with a gesture of impatience.

"Did you ever see *The Poseidon Adventure*? The original, with Gene Hackman?" Iris motioned to the window. "If I get stuck, it'll take the fire department an hour to saw me out."

They heard a thumping from overhead that might have been the wind or might have been something else. "Fine, I'll go in and unlock the door," said Geneva. "You wait here."

Ascending the low hill toward the window, Geneva stuck her head in and wriggled through without much effort. She found herself in a narrow, cramped room smelling of floor cleaner and disinfectant, containing a row of vending machines and several desks and chairs. A door stood to her left which led out into a long hallway. Geneva opened the door at the back of the hallway and found Iris still waiting below on the slick sidewalk.

"Come on," said Geneva, "I'm afraid we may not have much time."

Grabbing hold of the railing, Iris began to make her way up. But then—it all happened so quickly—just as she reached the third step, she slipped and with a loud cry that must have echoed into the building fell back and landed flat on her back.

For an awful moment she lay there, writhing and twisting like some over-sized insect and moaning apologetically. Carefully—very carefully—Geneva descended the stairs and knelt down beside her.

"Iris," she said quietly; for the moment, all thought of the intruder upstairs were forgotten. "Iris, dear, are you alright?"

Iris took her hand in hers. "I'm not dying, if that's what you mean." There was an unsettling blankness in her voice, and some of the color seemed to be leaving her face. "I think I could come with you, if you just give me a moment."

"Can you move, though?" said Geneva. She had a sudden, horrible vision of Iris being confined to a hospital bed for the rest of your life. "Your legs, can you still move them?"

Iris kicked her left leg out, and then her right. She smiled weakly; Geneva could sense she was making a game attempt to look braver than she was. "Body's in proper shape. Honestly, I think I could go for a dance."

Geneva ignored her. "Listen, I'm going to help carry you back to the car. I don't want to hear any fuss. I've got to go in there, and you're in no state to be going with me."

Iris nodded in resignation, perhaps sensing once again that it would be useless to argue. "I don't know if I can walk on my own yet," she said, "but I swear to you, Gen, if you go up there and get murdered, I'll storm heaven and kill you again."

It was another ten minutes before Geneva managed to get Iris comfortably seated in the purple station wagon. As she strode back through the *Beacon*'s parking lot in the direction of the back entrance, she made a third attempt to call the police station. When this failed, she dialed Gerry's personal cell, which she had been warned to use only in the event of emergencies—but again, there was no answer.

Carefully Geneva returned up the steps into the building, using her phone as a light to guide her through the hallway. Whoever was lurking up there would undoubtedly have heard Iris's yell, perhaps even seen them skulking in and out of the parking lot through a window and would either be hastening their exit or preparing themselves for her arrival.

She paused at the door to the elevator, deliberating. The second she pressed the button, the chime of the bell would resound in the silence. No, best if she took the stairs. Ducking into one of the empty offices, she fumbled around on the desk and eventually landed on a stapler, which she grabbed and carried with her as she entered the stairwell. Iris had been right: it would make no sense to venture up there unarmed, and her self-defense classes—if they had taught her nothing else—had revealed how even the most ordinary object could be wielded like a weapon.

Midway between the first floor and the fourth she paused to catch her breath in a patch of moonlight streaming in through a narrow un-curtained window. The loneliness of the moment would have overwhelmed her if she had thought too hard about it, but Geneva charged ahead, fearing that she was making an awful ruckus with the slamming of doors and the echo of her boots on the stairs. It was with a sense of relief mingled with dread that she opened the door looking out onto the fourth-floor hallway, half-expecting a knife-wielding maniac to leap out at her from the shadows.

But there was no one. No noise, nothing.

Taking off her boots at the door, she glided soundlessly down the hallway. The thought flashed across her mind that maybe this had all been a trap, that Serenity had ginned up an imaginary danger and lured her up here on purpose in the hope of getting rid of her. But then, Serenity had had no way of knowing that she would be coming alone...

She hadn't thought to ask which of the many doors lining this hallway led into the main office, but she didn't have to—towards the middle of the hallway stood a room vast and cavernous, considerably larger than any of the other rooms she had passed, its double doors open, illuminated by moonlight and streetlight beaming in from floor-to-ceiling windows looking out over the McDonald's parking lot and the Greyhound bus station beyond. There was no sign of any intruder. Drawing her breath like a woman diving, Geneva inched forward into the office—

The attack, when it came, was sudden and brutal. Geneva felt a blow to her gut that left her winded even before she was flung to the floor. Someone must have been standing behind the door—standing, waiting, with all the patience and fortitude of a spider, hardly daring to breathe. As the first shock subsided and Geneva recovered her vision, she could see him looming over her, smiling horribly, with his round cherubic face and thinning air putting her in mind of an angel thrown out of heaven.

"Mr. Overton," she said lightly, with that air of politeness which infuriated so many. "Wasn't expecting to see you here."

"Try being my age; I wasn't expecting to see a lot of things," said Mr. Overton, grabbing her roughly by the arm and beginning to pull her to her feet. Serenity had spoken the truth: in the palm of his right hand, he held a long kitchen knife, the blade of which glinted in the light from the window. "Get up. Did you bring anyone with you?"

"Not a soul," said Geneva coolly, eyeing the stapler which lay ten yards away, near the water cooler. "You?"

Mr. Overton shook his head. "Roman isn't helping me, if that's what you're thinking. If you want anything done properly in this world, you've got to do it yourself." He held the knife just under her chin, not quite sharp enough to draw blood; Geneva winced, nonetheless. "If I find anyone else in this building..."

He didn't finish the sentence; he didn't have to. This simple statement had, however, told Geneva more than he had intended. He still wasn't aware that Serenity was lurking somewhere in the back of the office. Perhaps that was for the best. Better one of them die than both.

"March," said Mr. Overton gruffly, pulling her forward, and together, they strode to the windows on the opposite end of the room.

From here, Geneva could see much of downtown—the local CVS, the parking garage next to the city's main library, a sidewalk slick with half-melted snow. There was, she could see now, a sort of tranquil beauty to the whole scene; at the same instant, it occurred to her that she might be looking at it for the last time.

"I don't suppose you're going to tell me why you're here," said Geneva.

"I don't see any reason to keep it secret," said Mr. Overton plainly, "as I don't intend on letting you go."

Geneva said nothing. She had known criminals who used threats as a bluff, never intending to follow through. Mr. Overton wasn't one of those. She had no doubt that he was prepared to use the knife and any other means at his disposal to guarantee her permanent silence. He radiated a sense that at any moment he might plunge the blade into her neck.

"That awful reporter," he said, "that ogress, has in her possession pictures of me that were taken at the visitation of Madeline Ponderphelt. I had driven down there, posing as a childhood friend, to ensure that her death hadn't aroused any undue suspicions. I was relieved to see that pretty much everyone believed she had taken her own life. But then as I stood by the coffin"—and here he balled his fists—"little Miss Mind-Your-Business snapped a picture of me. I've been trying to get it back ever since."

"But there must have been others who saw you," said Geneva, wanting to put off the moment of her death for as long as she could. "Madeline wasn't the only woman you killed."

"No, there was that other reporter, the obituary writer." It was cold enough in the office that he shivered as he spoke. "She made the mistake of posting on Facebook, of all places, that something about Madeline's death wasn't adding up. Then she started digging around, and like Madeline before her, discovered the scam I was running."

Geneva sensed she was pushing her luck now, but couldn't help asking, "What scam?"

"Aren't you just full of questions?" said Mr. Overton, but then added, "About a year ago, I was down on Sixth Street on a Friday evening when Cherry Bobbins, the actress, had a drunken meltdown in front of Grommand's Diner. I managed to record about three minutes of footage on my phone and very quickly posted it to Twitter, where it went viral."

He laughed, though it was a laugh from which all real joy seemed to have vanished. "I started hanging out around downtown, snapping photos and video footage of bigwigs in compromising positions. That went on for several months with no trouble."

Evidently relishing his captive audience, Mr. Overton waited for her to ask, "What happened?"

"What happened is that I was hit with a cease-and-desist letter," he said angrily, "from lawyers representing Lucky Mittens. On top of all that, I was bleeding money. My prize truck was on the brink of repossession. It was time for a different tack. The answer came to me one morning while I was reading one of Roman Koistinen's books on how to write a mystery thriller. He mentioned blackmail, and it occurred to me that I was sitting on a veritable goldmine with all the incriminating photos I possessed."

"You began squeezing people in secret," said Geneva.

"That's it!" Mr. Overton cried with gusto. "You wouldn't believe the sheer *number* of people in this town whose secrets I'm holding onto. If I wanted, I could empty City Hall tomorrow. Rich folk will happily pay you to keep their pristine reputations intact. That old widower whom I caught with an escort—"

"Yes, what about him?" said Geneva, with a feeling of revulsion at the pure glee in his face.

"He was almost *relieved* when he figured out it was just a shakedown, that all I wanted was money. We had the transaction over and done in ten minutes. I feel like an idiot for having spent all those years laboring away in obscurity for pennies."

"I try to be wary of any scheme that promises to bring me easy cash," said Geneva coolly. "That's a rule I've always lived by, and it's never steered me wrong yet."

"No, but it hasn't made you rich, either," said Mr. Overton in a paternal tone. "And look at it this way: if you had more money, you wouldn't be having to sleuth around town in the middle of the night, and your life wouldn't have tragically come to an abrupt end."

Placing the tip of the knife at her back and jerking her forward, so that she let out a little shriek of terror, Mr. Overton grabbed her by the hair. "Sorry we couldn't get a better view," he said, "but you had better take a final look, because this is the last thing you're ever gonna see."

"My partner has called the police," said Geneva with a hopeless feeling. "They're on their way."

"You're lying," said Mr. Overton, unruffled. "The line's busy; it's been busy all night. You wanna know how I know? Because I called the place myself."

He jabbed the tip of the knife even deeper into her back. Geneva steeled herself, not wanting to give him the satisfaction of hearing her scream. "Now because you're a nice lady, and you remind me of my mom, I'm going to let you say a final prayer—"

There was a blur of motion and a clang of metal, and Mr. Overton collapsed like a stone thrown into water. So great was Geneva's shock that for a moment she could only gaze upon him lying there, his head pressed against the window, reminding her irresistibly of a little boy sleeping.

Then her rescuer stepped forward out of the shadows, clutching a shovel in one hand and glowering at Mr. Overton with the same look of contempt that she had often given Geneva in school.

"I don't guess he'll be waking up for a while," said Joanne. "How late are the bars in this town open on weeknights? Do you want to go out and grab a drink?"

"B-but how on earth did you come to be here?" Geneva asked, stunned that Joanne had actually spoken to her.

"Your friend, Iris. She was desperate. Said the police weren't answering…"

Geneva grinned. Good ole Iris.

[12]

They managed to find one pub in all of Wrangler's that was still happen, a shabby one-room unit with a brick interior and tacky busts of Golden Age film stars (James Stewart, Marilyn Monroe) made up to look like Greek gods and goddesses. Geneva texted George to invite him over. Within ten minutes, he strode through the door wearing his battered fedora and sat down in the booth next to Iris, who was feeling well enough to order drinks for herself and everyone present.

"What happened to the killer?" asked George, opening a packet of sweetener and letting it snow down into his Bloody Mary. "Surely you didn't just leave him there?"

"We handcuffed him to a radiator," said Geneva proudly. "Serenity happened to have a pair of handcuffs on hand, no telling how. Luckily, Iris had already gotten hold of the police and they came charging in about ten minutes later."

"They swarmed me," said Joanne. "Because I was holding a shovel, I think they assumed I was the killer."

"Why were you still holding the shovel?" asked Iris.

"In case Vince woke up again," she replied.

The pub remained open until twelve. Geneva bought the second round of drinks and Joanne the third. Serenity bowed out after the second round, saying she needed to get home.

"It's been lovely, though," she said. "It's a weird feeling, having friends."

By this point, Iris had drunk herself into a sleepy stupor and was dozing fitfully with her head leaned back against the vinyl upholstery, which was peeling in places. George was singing "Whale of a Tale" to himself in a melancholy tone as he stirred his gin and tonic, as if lamenting a lost love.

"Strange to be reconnecting after all this time," said Joanne. "Frankly I didn't think it was ever going to happen."

"Nor did I," said Geneva sadly. "I'd given you up for dead ages ago."

An especially fierce wind battered at the window and the door flew open, snow drifting in and settling on the tiles as if awaiting its turn for drinks. The bartender, a middle-aged gentleman who looked as though he had recently given himself a haircut and made a bad job of it, trotted over and closed the door and double-bolted it.

"Not letting anyone else in here tonight," he said. "But you lot can stay as long as you'd like."

Geneva signaled her appreciation and went on studying Joanne's face. "What made you do it? Come to our rescue, I mean?"

Joanne didn't seem to be entirely sure herself. "It seems a bit ridiculous, doesn't it? Carrying a schoolgirl grudge into late middle age?" She gazed down at her glass with a bleak expression. "None of us are the same people we were at the age of seventeen. I figure it would be wrong to continue to hold you to account for something that was done to me nearly forty years ago. You were a different person, then."

"You seem to have grown up quite a bit yourself," said Geneva.

Joanne nodded. "Well, one would hope. I'm not particularly proud of everything I did at that age, either. I'm not saying I'm glad you snitched... but I don't know, maybe I had it coming."

"I still shouldn't have done it," said Geneva, adjusting her shoulder onto which George had fallen and was now snoring softly. "It's not as though I really cared about the integrity of the paper. I wanted the editor's position for myself, pure and simple. I'd have done anything to get it."

"Well, we had that in common, at least," Joanne replied, and for a long while they sat there in silence.

Perhaps it was the lateness of the hour, or perhaps the beer was making Geneva unusually sad and reflective; but as they went on looking at each other from across the table Geneva couldn't help thinking of the years she had missed by sabotaging her early friendship with Joanne. Half a lifetime had passed since they had last spoken—Geneva had enjoyed a whole career; had acquired and lost a husband. And yet somehow, forty years didn't seem that long ago. Perhaps they weren't as far from being young as they liked to think.

"You know, I never hated you," said Joanne, not quite looking at her. "I was just *so hurt* after you ratted on me. It felt like the ultimate betrayal. I think it would have hurt less if we had hated each other before. But you were my friend, and then you weren't. And I guess it was easier just to be angry, because then I didn't have to contend with any deeper feelings."

"I'm sorry, Joanne," said Geneva. "Afterward, I didn't even want to be editor, not really."

"I'm just sorry that I let it come between us for so long," Joanne replied. "At least once a year I would look you up on Facebook, think about sending you a message, and then..."

"I thought about it, as well, on and off. I didn't think you wanted to hear from me. I had no idea where you were."

George let out a loud snore and sat up slowly, blinking back confusion. "Land sakes, how much did I drink?" he asked.

"More than you should have," Geneva said with a bemused smile. "Suffice it to say, I'll be the one driving us home tonight in your car. We'll probably have to come back for Iris's car in the morning, or whenever the weather clears."

Iris stirred, opened one eye, then closed it again. "I don't want to watch *Citizen Kane*..." she murmured sleepily and turned over on her side.

"No, I'm definitely not letting her drive home tonight," said Geneva. She unbuttoned her woolen coat and laid it gingerly across Iris's chest. Instinctively, Iris burrowed into it with a contented look, bringing to mind a mole inside a cozy tunnel.

"Maybe we ought to let her sleep," said Geneva. "She's had a rough couple of weeks, between slip-sliding down the stairs tonight and getting thrown out of the gardening club."

"Did they ever get that sorted?" asked George.

"Yes, as it turns out, bullying Iris was the only thing holding that little club together." Since Iris had left, the other women in the club had all turned on each other in a series of purges. Gladys and Flora were the only ones left, and each had declared the other expelled in perpetuity.

"Iris will be fine, I think," said Geneva. "The question in front of us now is, how are we going to get her back to the car?"

"Maybe let her sleep a bit longer?" said George. "I don't see that we have to leave right away."

Geneva motioned to the window, against which the snow was now steadily falling. "George, dear, have you seen the world? I say the sooner we get home, the better."

"Rubbish," said George, and draining the last of his glass, he rose and headed for the bar. "You can sap all the joy if you want, but I'm getting another drink, and not you or anyone else—"

He never finished the sentence, however, for at that moment every light in the building went out, leaving him and the three women in total darkness.

The End

CONTINUE READING…

Thank you for reading *SLANDER **& Psychics!*** Are you wondering **what to read next?** Why not read ***Valentine Balloons & Bodies?*** **Here's a sneak peek for you:**

It was an achingly cold February morning, the sort of cold where even tights and two layers of socks weren't protection enough against the nipping air. A small shower of snow dislodged itself from the eaves of the house and drifted down in a flurry as Geneva Pomolo—fifty-eight, ruddy-cheeked, with greying hair and thick-rimmed glasses—flung open the front door.

"It's an outrage," she said. "This woman obviously doesn't know anything about me, or she wouldn't be running her mouth like this."

Her housemate, Iris Reeves, came trotting in behind her carrying a paper bag full of groceries in each arm and looking slightly flustered and out of breath. George Wilson, Geneva's gentleman friend, pressed pause on the TV and rose sleepily from the couch. "Who said what now?" he asked.

"Don't get her started," said Iris in an ominous tone. "Gen, you were a teacher. You should know better than to let the manic ravings of some old lady get to you."

"If it were a student, it wouldn't have bothered me," said Geneva, angrily pulling a head of lettuce from a plastic wrapper and plopping it down on the kitchen table. "But Gladys is in charge of party planning at church—she's married to the assistant pastor—"

"What did she say?" asked George, with boyish impatience. "You can't just leave me hanging."

Iris slipped on a pair of yellow rubber gloves and began tying up the garbage bag by the corners. "All Gladys said," remarked Iris, "is that she thinks Gen is a little too 'sedentary' and 'set in her ways—'"

"*Hopelessly dull and out of touch* were her exact words," said Geneva, brandishing several stalks of green onions. "One would think the past three to four years hadn't even happened."

"Admittedly, her description could not have been further from the reality," said Iris. "It's a bit like describing the reign of Oliver Cromwell as 'largely peaceful.'" Iris beamed proudly, as she did whenever she made a reference to an event in English history.

"Is she familiar with your work?" asked George, looking quite surprised.

For the past three to four years, ever since her retirement from public teaching, Geneva had been working as a private investigator—in which capacity she had been stabbed, shot at, flung from the roof of a high-rise and nearly killed by a leopard. Geneva's doctor had warned her that the strain of constant exertion could irreparably damage her body, but Geneva didn't seem to have heard him.

Click Here to Continue Reading!

https://ticahousepublishing.com/cozy-mystery.html

IF YOU LOVE COZY MYSTERIES, **Click Here**

https://cozymystery.subscribemenow.com/

to hear about all **New Donna Muse Mystery Releases! I will let you know as soon as they become available!**

Thank you, Friends! If you enjoyed *Slander & Psychics,* would you kindly take a couple minutes to leave a positive review on Amazon? It only takes a moment, and positive reviews truly make a difference. Thank you so much! I appreciate it!

Much love,

Donna Muse

ABOUT THE AUTHOR

Donna Muse has been a mystery buff for years! But she hasn't been a fan of blood and gore. So when the Cozy Mystery genre came into being, she jumped on board with both feet. She loves the amateur sleuth and is fascinated by the intense and often comical way the perpetrator is revealed. Donna lives in Maine with her husband, loves walking by the surf, fishing for striped bass, and playing with her grandchildren and her cats.

contact@ticahousepublishing.com